When she turned to walk away, he grabbed her hand and pulled. At the same time he swept his leg around to knock her off her feet. As she tumbled, he positioned his body under hers and rolled with her so that he was on top and she was pinned beneath him.

"First you want to use me for bait," he growled. "Then you don't care if I die alongside you. Nice."

"You're not my concern. Killing Skinwalkers, killing the Wolf. That's all that matters."

"Like hell. If you think that, you're nothing but a monster like they are." He held her arms down and got right in her face.

"You matter," he said in a hoarse whisper. "What's there between us matters."

Dear Reader,

And so we come to the conclusion of the NIGHT GUARDIANS series. This is the story of Sunnie Begay, the nurse from *Shadow Watch,* who had been tricked by her fiancé, the Skinwalker. Now she's a woman on a mission—to find and kill the Navajo Wolf! She meets Cisco Santiago, a man on his own mission, and from their first encounter sparks fly.

I just love this emotional story about two damaged spirits trying to uncover secrets. I sincerely hope you've enjoyed reading all the NIGHT GUARDIANS as much as I have writing about them!

Here are a few Navajo words to help with your understanding:

Dine	The Navajo—also known as The People
Dinetah	The land between the four sacred mountains where legend says the Dine began (the Four-Corners Big reservation, encompassing parts of Arizona, New Mexico, Colorado and Utah)
anali	grandmother (paternal)
bilagaana	white (as in "white man")
chindi	the dark spirits who come with death
hastiin	mister, the title for a respected clan elder
hataalii	medicine man
hogan	the traditional housing of the Navajo, built in an eight-sided design—now mostly used for religious purposes
hozho	harmony/balance
Naakaii	the Mexican clan people
ya'at'eeh	hello
Yei	the gods of Navajo myths

Enjoy!

Linda Conrad

Linda Conrad

SHADOW WHISPERS

Silhouette®

Romantic

SUSPENSE

SILHOUETTE BOOKS

ISBN-13: 978-0-373-27551-9
ISBN-10:   0-373-27551-X

SHADOW WHISPERS

Visit Silhouette Books at www.eHarlequin.com

Printed in U.S.A.

LINDA CONRAD

Linda Conrad was inspired by her mother, who gave her a deep love of storytelling. "Mom told me I was the best liar she ever knew. And that's saying something for a woman with an Irish storyteller's background," Linda says. Linda has been writing contemporary romances for Silhouette Books for six years. Besides telling stories, her passions are her husband and family, and finding the time to read cozy mysteries and emotional love stories. Linda keeps busy and is happy living in the sunshine near the Florida Keys. Visit Linda's Web site at www.lindaconrad.com.

Chapter 1

Like a panther, she stalked her prey through the shivery, silent night. The young Navajo woman going by the name Sunnie Begay had made herself too tough to feel the cold. *Other forces* made her too tough to care.

Alone but bolstered by the knowledge and expertise she had recently acquired, Sunnie crept through sagebrush and granite boulders. Too dark on this moonless night to see much, she let her memory, honed senses and imagination guide the way.

As she edged ever so surely to her date with destiny, instinct told her that at last the end was near.

Tonight she would catch the Navajo Wolf unawares. She would take her shot, ending the misery the People had for years endured at the hands of that abomination of mankind. The monster who had wreaked his last bit of suffering on Navajoland would go the way he had lived—through violence.

Hefting the rifle case that had become her only companion over the last six months, Sunnie took her spot among the rocks. On this blustery winter's evening, the last of the cottonwood leaves rattled in the frosty midnight hours.

She carefully removed her dismantled rifle from the case and admired its shiny barrel by the light of the stars. Using her teeth, she pulled off her sheepskin gloves and caught the faint scent of gun oil. Listening to the intense quiet of the desert and the cliffs surrounding her position, Sunnie took each measured step with noiseless deliberation.

As her fingers trailed over the polished mahogany stock, she considered how far she had come. An unlikely assassin, she was nevertheless a dedicated and proficient one. Over the last six months she'd taken what used to be a happy childhood hobby of target practice and turned it into a deadly vocation.

She'd made herself over from a young rifle target shooter into a crack shot. A sniper who, with the right equipment, could put a bullet through the eye of a needle as it traveled at seventy miles per hour.

But a needle was not her intended target. Not tonight. Not ever.

The only target she ever intended to see down the barrel of her nightscope was the leader of the Skinwalkers: the Navajo Wolf. The man who had taken many lives and destroyed countless others. Seeing to his destruction was now her sole mission.

Her previous life was long gone. Friends, family and old occupations had been ripped away. Her future looked every bit as bleak as her current life.

But for tonight she had found a valid reason to take each breath. For tonight—for just a little while longer. Until it was done.

Until the Navajo Wolf was no more.

Cisco Santiago would've killed for a shot of tequila right about now. The day had been long and was getting longer. In fact, the moonless night looked about ready to give way to dawn. So, actually, he supposed it was already tomorrow.

Still, he was sure the man whose SUV he followed would eventually lead him to the next piece in the puzzle. And that was worth a missed night's sleep and a lost meal or two.

The road under his vehicle's wheels had turned to gravel about a mile back. And the landscaping—what little he could see of it by the stars—had taken on an eerie feeling of otherworldliness. His senses turned edgy. But though he remained alert, he wasn't worried.

The young Navajo man had claimed to have a relative in the desert who might be a reliable informant. But after watching the kid down several drinks in that bar in Farmington, New Mexico, Cisco had listened when his gut told him to drive his own car.

His Charger, sleek on the outside but all V-8 hemi power on the inside, usually got him in and out of most tight spots. But perhaps tonight, what with the blackness of the night and the narrow gravel road, traveling in the other guy's four-wheel-drive would've been the smarter move.

There was nothing in life Cisco hadn't tried and little he didn't dare, including walking into some kind of setup. High risks were merely the potential for high reward. It was what had brought him the most success in his life. What had taken a poor barrio kid and turned him into a successful entrepreneur. Into a man who wielded enormous authority and respect, even in a chosen profession that normally invited neither.

But Cisco was good at what he did and he liked being a high-powered skip tracer. "Bounty-hunter" was how he would be viewed in some less knowledgeable people's minds. The bounty he usually hunted, though, was far more refined and intelligent and much harder to catch than the average person knew.

Skip tracers worked for bail bondsmen. Cisco's company did both bonding and tracing. Someone needed to bring in the errant white-collar criminals who had chosen flight instead of justice. The police were always glad to have help bringing their criminals back from overseas.

That's where he was the best, and where his employees excelled. He now had a dozen operatives, most of whom could be trusted to find and retrieve their quarries anywhere in the world. His businesses also employed crack international bankers and a raft of lawyers. Finding rich runaway criminals was usually a lot easier when you tracked their bank accounts rather than their actual movements.

The road beneath his car suddenly curved, and Cisco

automatically checked his rearview mirror to make sure no one was following. He saw nothing but his own brown eyes in the dim backglow from his headlights. He'd flipped off the dashboard lights earlier in order to better navigate in the pitch-black of such a remote area. But now he couldn't even see the rest of his face in the mirror.

Cisco worked on shutting down his growing tension by practicing the things that had made him the fearsome tracker. He prided himself in being able to give verbal descriptions of people's physical attributes after only cursory inspections. He could call up vivid descriptions better than police sketch artists.

In his head he listed the physical description of the Navajo he'd been following. A six-foot, strapping twenty-something, the kid wasn't anything special in his jeans and all-weather jacket. His short, dark brown hair matched the deep-set brown-black eyes. In fact, the eyes were the only standout in the whole description, and that was because of the vacant, almost dead look in them. Cisco had seen some drugged-out gazes in his time, but the look in this kid's eyes was something he had never beheld.

Cisco gave up trying to catalog it and began listing his own description—or the description of the desperado he had worked so hard to become.

The lean, six-two body of a dangerous man, usually clad in black jeans and leather jacket. The slightly too long ebony hair. The day-old stubble covering a jutting chin and slashing cheekbones. The brown and burnished-toned skin that spoke of a Mexican-American heritage. And the perpetual sneer that frequently pulled at the too-full lips and the razor-thin white scar at the side of his mouth.

The scar was real and only one of many. He'd received it in a knife fight when he was a teenager. Women loved the scars. Men respected them.

But the rest of the menacing image was meant for the mean streets. He had deliberately designed it to be a hundred and eighty degrees from the real man underneath. Cisco had gone way back to his hard roots to cultivate the perfect looks and image of the dangerous Latino *hombre*. A bounty hunter who never lost his man under any circumstances.

The real Cisco preferred fine wine and rare first editions. He'd call himself a refined new-age man who'd earned a master's degree in Art History. A self-taught man of the world who could discuss the Chinese philosophers and would easily win a debate on nearly any subject.

The road ahead made another wide turn around the base of a cliff, and he remembered his true mission for this trip. Business wasn't what had brought him to the Navajo reservation tonight. No, this was personal. And long overdue.

Soon he would uncover the answers he'd sought for most of his life. Now that he had the time and the money to make things happen, nothing would stop him from learning the truth.

The winds had finally died down as Sunnie took great pains fitting together the rifle components, then loading the shells into the chamber with a quiet snap. Caressing the sleek metal and warm wood as she went, she studied each piece. Testing, she tightened her finger lightly against the trigger, then lifted it again.

The rifle had become like her child, to be petted and admired. It was a replacement for the baby she had once imagined she would have. But that was in another lifetime—before her fiancé betrayed her and sold her spirit to the Skinwalkers.

Louis Singleton, the fiancé she had once loved and then grown to hate, had paid for sins against his own people. Paid with his life, like all who failed the Wolf. But she too had paid, in lost dreams, shattered hopes and months of reprogramming by the Brotherhood.

Thank the gods for the Brotherhood. Without them, the Dine would be lost against their evil enemies. And she would've been lost, as well.

The Brotherhood had rescued her, given her shelter and, in the end, a kind of peace. Though their efforts proved to be only a temporary reprieve from the horrors of the night.

She now knew the truth: there could be no real peace. Not for her. Not until the Wolf was dead. Maybe not ever.

Taking up her position, Sunnie waited. The night became timeless, the strain and tension on her body unheeded. She was ready to cope with any physical test.

For weeks now she had watched and waited. Tracing patterns, seeing similarities.

From an earlier time, she remembered this particular place. The canyon road below her was on the Navajo Wolf's route when he moved around the reservation. She was the only one alive to know his custom was to travel the gravel road but only in the dead of night. Oftentimes he traveled as the Wolf. There would be little opportunity for taking a shot while he was in that superhuman condition.

Would he come this time in human form and by car? If so, would it be in a caravan of comrades or all alone in his black sedan?

The Navajo Wolf's minutes on earth were numbered. Sunnie didn't care how many protectors surrounded him. He didn't stand a chance against her marksmanship.

The Wolf would not be expecting such an ambush in Navajoland. It was not the sort of thing any traditionally trained Navajo would do. Not even the Brotherhood would attempt an out-and-out assassination.

Sunnie's own mother, a traditional Navajo, would have been mortified to think of her only daughter doing anything so out of character, regardless of how badly her family had been treated by the demon of the night. Traditional Dine did not seek revenge—or even punishment—for those who had lost the true Way. They sought only to rehabilitate the offender to harmony, restoring the balance within them and to their clan.

But her mother had died when Sunnie was a teen, before the current Skinwalker threat had come to Dinetah. Sunnie now thought of her mother's early death to cancer as a blessing. It had protected her from witnessing the ugly horror that had befallen her family and clan.

And it had shielded her mother from the truth of what her only daughter had become: a cold, calculating killer. A woman whose only purpose in life came down to one shot.

Sunnie knew the Brotherhood believed she was still

safely hidden away with her new identity. And her real brothers thought she had left Dinetah long ago, as they had. Today there were few friends and no other family left to wonder about Sunnie Begay's whereabouts and motives.

Which should have been a sentimental thought, but Sunnie felt nothing. Nothing but the growing urgency to make that one shot.

Then it was there. The faint buzz that had become known to the Brotherhood as the announcement of a pending Skinwalker appearance.

She noticed a slight tension running across her shoulders and deliberately forced them down. There would be no mistakes tonight. No chance of letting the Wolf get away to wreak havoc on the Dine for another day.

"Come on, you bastard. Drive into your destiny."

Through the darkness two pairs of headlights appeared around the curve that circumvented Hawk's Way Bluff. She peered through her nightscope. A light-colored SUV led the way. The dark sedan followed closely behind.

"No way, monster. No bodyguard in any SUV will protect you this night. You are mine."

Lightly squeezing her finger against the trigger, Sunnie watched through her nightscope and began tracking the sedan. Waiting. Anticipating the right moment.

She smelled the snakeweed and gnarled juniper of the desert around her. Felt the warmth of polished wood beneath her cheek. This was her moment. There would be no wind to contend with. No innocent bystanders to interfere.

Seconds clicked by as the sedan crept ever closer. Then he was there in her scope. Alone and driving.

Her brain processed all the variables as her finger squeezed ever tighter. In the brightness of the infrared light through her scope she caught the same arrogant chin, the same sharp jawline she remembered from the times she'd seen the Wolf in person.

Ten more feet… She took her shot.

But at the last possible moment Sunnie realized what she'd really been seeing. The man in her scope was a good twenty to thirty years younger than the monster she sought. The skin under this guy's stubble was not pockmarked. The thick hair was a touch too long and much too ebony.

The man behind the wheel was not her target. Not the Navajo Wolf.

Too late, she tried to deflect the bullet. Twitching her hand on the barrel, she knew before she looked up that it was not enough. The shot had already met its mark.

She watched in horror as the sedan slowed, then ran off the road. It disappeared behind an outcropping of boulders.

Looking toward the east, she half expected to find the SUV slowing and turning back to see what had happened to its companion. Instead the four-wheel-drive disappeared around the next curve in the road. Perhaps the big vehicle would have to find a wider place to turn around.

She checked over her shoulder, anticipating some kind of Skinwalker retaliation. But nothing stirred.

What had she done? Who had she shot?

Who had she killed?

Sunnie stealthily slipped across the gravel road, rifle in hand. She had to know for sure. This might be a more dangerous move even than a planned assassination of the Wolf, but she had to find out if the man she'd shot was truly dead.

She had driven her old Jeep down the less steep side of the canyon and parked it about a half mile back up the road, out of sight. The whole time she'd been fully prepared to meet up with the SUV and whatever Skinwalker had been driving it. But there was no sign of anything.

What would she find behind the boulders? Had the Skinwalkers changed forms and flown back to take away their own? Would the sedan be empty when she got there? Or would the whole vehicle have disappeared into the fog of evil that surrounded it?

Tightening her grip on the rifle, she flattened her body against the granite and inched into the shadows behind the rocks. The gray cast of dawn was beginning to lighten the shadows now, and there would be no place to hide if a confrontation with the Skinwalkers took place.

She knew it was only a matter of time.

Surprised to find the sedan sitting with its nose smashed against the base of the bluff, Sunnie was actually glad to see that it had not been spirited away. However, she was also terrified. The Skinwalkers could still be on their way back.

In a hurry now, she peered through the bullet-shattered side window and saw a man's body squished between the seat back and the deployed air bag. There seemed to be blood on every interior surface of the front seat.

She stepped closer to get a better look at her unintended target. One step. Two.

Then she heard it. A moan. The man was alive.

Without giving her own safety a second thought, Sunnie dropped the rifle, ripped open the driver's door and quickly felt his carotid artery for a pulse. Once a nurse, always a nurse, she supposed.

Surprisingly his pulse was strong under her fingers. Where had her bullet entered his body? The blood seemed most prevalent around his head. Her aim had been the temple, but that was not likely what she'd hit.

Thank the *Yei*. Her last-second deflection had worked. She hadn't killed him.

"Can you move? Can you tell me where it hurts?"

The man groaned as his head fell back against the seat. He was trying to be responsive but was too groggy. Sunnie figured it was a good sign. At least he wasn't out cold.

Searching for the wound, Sunnie took his face in her hands and gently probed for the entry point. All she found was an open gap in the skin high on his forehead, where her bullet had nicked him. The huge amount of blood was from the facial wound, nothing deadly. But apparently he had also hit his head on something during the car wreck.

She took off her jacket and ripped out the hem of her T-shirt. Placing the bunched material against his wound, she tried to halt the blood flow.

"What else hurts? Anything broken? Can you move?" Suddenly Sunnie wanted more than anything to get away from the sedan. But she would never leave him this way.

"N-no. My head is all that hurts. Nothing else." The man blinked a couple of times but seemed unable to focus. "What happened?"

"I… You were shot and your car ran off the road. We

need to move you from behind that air bag so I can check for other injuries. Do you think you can help me get you out of the car?"

"Shot?" The man finally opened his eyes, and Sunnie fought the urge to gasp. A dangerous dark brown gaze watched her intently in the dawn's first light.

Who was this man? She could see he was not Navajo, so his being a Skinwalker was an impossibility. But what was he doing out here in the dark hours before dawn, following the Skinwalker route?

She slid her free arm between his body and the seat back, urging him gently to move. "Come on. It's only a surface wound. I'll help you stand. We have to go."

The man twisted his body awkwardly and put his feet on the ground beside the door. "Are we in danger? Is the car on fire?"

They *were* in danger but not from anything to do with the car accident. And judging from his rugged appearance and arrogant stare, Sunnie wasn't so sure this man might not turn out to be even more dangerous for her. She couldn't be sure of anything until she knew who he really was.

"No danger of fire. What are you doing out here at night? Who are you?" she demanded in a loud whisper.

"Cisco," he mumbled. "Francisco Santiago. And you?"

"What happened to that SUV you were following?" she insisted without answering his question. "Did your buddies abandon you?"

He started to shake his head but groaned instead and leaned into his open palm. "Man, my head is foggy. What did you say your name was?"

"Sunnie," she said. There was no reason to give him her real name. Not when she'd been living under an assumed one for the last year. "Sunnie Begay."

She couldn't be sure, but the faint sound of the Skinwalker buzz seemed to grow in the distance. "If you're not expecting that SUV to come back for you, we need to get out of here."

"Expecting…? No. I don't even know that guy's name. I was supposed to follow him to his clan's hogan to meet with somebody else."

"Whose hogan exactly? What was the clan name?"

"I don't know that, either. Sorry." He lifted his chin and looked at her. "I think I can stand now. Why are we in such a hurry to move?"

"I'll explain it to you later." She helped him hang on to the sedan's roof as he eased his way to a standing position. "You're sure nothing else hurts? Not your ribs or anything in the chest cavity?"

"Are you a doctor?"

"A waitress. Talk to me. Where does it hurt?"

"Except for what seems like a lot of blood and a monumental headache, I think I'm okay."

She gave him a quick check and found no other cuts or obvious broken bones. "My Jeep is back down the road about a half a mile. Do you think you can make it that far?"

"Probably. But I'm not sure I want to leave my car and all my stuff. Where are we going?"

"I have a friend with a clinic nearby. I want to get you checked over. Maybe put some stitches in that cut on your head. We'll send someone back in the daylight for your car and things." Sunnie bent and picked up her rifle, then put her arm around his waist to steady him as they walked.

He eyed the rifle, then tilted his head to her. "How'd I get shot, anyway?"

She wanted to hedge but decided truth would be easier. "It was me. I shot you."

Chapter 2

"Oh, yeah?" As bad as his head hurt, Cisco didn't think it was wise to wait for explanations.

The dark-haired babe had just admitted to putting him in this condition. That was enough for now.

Grabbing her by the shoulders, he twisted her against his chest with one arm and used his elbow to hold her by the neck. And, in a smooth move, he relieved her of the rifle with the other hand.

But in an equally smooth reflex movement, she crammed her elbow into his chin and dug her boot heel into the arch of his foot. The foot hurt like a bugger and was bad enough, but the crack to his chin had him seeing stars all over again.

Either she'd been trained in martial arts or he was a lot worse for wear from the gunshot and accident than he'd thought. She spun free; the rifle went flying, and he raised his arms to defend his head. She did the same and bent her knees in a fighter's stance.

"You need a doctor, you idiot," she said through gritted teeth. "Don't make me hurt you any more."

"Ha! Been there. It's me that doesn't want to hurt you." Hell, the little bitty thing couldn't be over five-three. He couldn't see himself punching her square in the face, even if she had shot him.

"Just let me keep the rifle. I think I have a right, don't you?" he demanded.

The answer he got was a swift kick to the kneecap. With a sharp crack and a roar of pain, he went down. But he managed enough presence of mind to roll toward her, grab her by the ankle and drag her crashing down to the ground on top of him. It was his advantage as he rolled her under him and imprisoned her with his more powerful and heavy body. She was fast. He was the elephant sitting on top of her.

"Let me up, you big freaking jerk," she squeaked breathlessly. "You're crushing me."

"Why'd you shoot me?"

"It'll take too long to give you an answer. We've got to get out of here. Now. Or we'll both end up shot—or worse."

Though he couldn't see her face clearly in the darkness, he could hear the growing panic in her voice. Something was going on here he didn't understand.

He had to make a few quick assumptions. The first was, if she'd really wanted to kill him, she could have easily done it while he'd been passed out in the car. The second was, the tiny beauty had to be Navajo. She knew much more about this world than he did. And, finally, his street instincts were screaming at him to pay attention to her warnings.

"Fine," he told her. "We'll go. But I still insist on carrying the rifle. Deal?"

She groaned and gave a halfhearted squirm, trying to break free. It only succeeded in making him suddenly aware of what was lying below him. A woman's body. Maybe a little too thin but certainly rounded in all the right places. That wasn't something he particularly wanted his own wounded body to be noticing at the moment.

"If you kill me, you won't make it out of the desert alive. You know that, right?" Her voice was getting breathy from the weight on her lungs.

"Right."

"Okay, then. Deal."

He didn't give her an opportunity to renege, but moved off her and bolted a few feet, grabbing the rifle on his way up. It wasn't that he needed another weapon—his was still in place under his jacket—but he sure as hell didn't want her to have the rifle again.

Positive whatever she'd intended with the shot had nothing to do with his personal mission to Navajoland, Cisco figured he had only been in the wrong place at the wrong time. But he was curious to know what she'd been after.

He also wanted to know why she didn't seem a bit concerned about being apprehended by the law for her assault. Didn't the Navajos have some kind of law against shooting people who were simply driving down the road? He would bet they did.

But she was obviously a Navajo, and he was just as obviously not one. This was her territory. Her laws. Her fight with some hidden force. He could imagine the local cops would all be on her side. But he sure as hell would find out. Just as soon as they reached civilization.

His curiosity grew stronger with every passing minute.

Cisco motioned her to start out ahead. "You lead. But stay close. It's not yet light out here, and I wouldn't want to shoot you in some important body part, like your head, when I couldn't see where I was aiming."

Before this day was over, he swore the woman would answer to him for her actions.

They walked silently back along the way he'd driven earlier. When they came to a bend in the road, she led him toward some scraggly juniper bushes. "Stay here a second while I check out the Jeep," she told him as they stopped behind a boulder.

"Why? What are you looking for?"

"Only being careful." Sunnie crept off into the gray light of dawn like an expert tracker.

Cisco's curiosity was expanding by the second as he kept his eye on her movements. What the hell was she so afraid of?

In five minutes she was back. "It's okay. Are you in a lot of pain?"

"No," he lied. "You drive. But no sudden moves I don't understand." He was glad for the chance to get off his feet again and maybe calm his queasy stomach.

Their ride to the "nearby" clinic turned into a forty-five-minute ordeal. Vast empty areas of reddish sand and rock sped by in the growing daylight, but he never saw another living soul. The wind rushing through the open vehicle was too noisy for conversation. And the January cold drove right through his clothes, chilling him to the bone.

Luckily the frigid temperatures were also numbing the pain in his head.

They finally arrived at a one-story building with a large parking lot that held only a handful of cars at this early hour. As they turned into the lot he carefully read the sign declaring the place was Raven Wash Medical Clinic. It looked much like most urgent-care facilities and small clinics he'd ever seen.

Sunnie parked in the back lot.

"Two things," he said as she turned off the engine. "Before we go inside, we're going to stow the rifle in that locker compartment behind the seats there. And then I'm going to call 911 and report the shooting and the accident while you sit quietly and wait. Any comments?"

She shook her head and folded her arms over her chest silently. But her expression said more than he wanted to hear. With the rising sun, he could clearly see her face. The nose was straight, the mouth firm and full. One smudge of dirt from their wrestling match creased her cheek right above a lopsided dimple.

And the eyes… He couldn't quite get a read on their color. Some shade of brown. But he could see that right this minute they were full of anger.

He placed the rifle in the open locker behind the seats. Then he pulled out his cell phone and dialed 911.

"Please state the nature of your emergency," the man who answered said.

"To whom am I speaking?" Cisco asked.

"This is the Navajo Nation Tribal Police emergency services. Do you have an emergency?"

"I'm calling to report a shooting and a car accident."

"State your name, and is anyone injured?"

Hmm. Maybe calling 911 had been the wrong thing to do. "The name's Cisco Santiago, and I'm injured. I was shot in the head."

"We'll send an ambulance. Where are you?"

"Uh, Raven Wash Medical Clinic. But…"

"You're at the clinic now?"

"Yeah, but…"

"If no one else is injured, have Dr. Wauneka report the shooting to us. We'll send someone over to take your statement."

"But wait. What about the shooter? I have her with…" The line had gone dead.

He turned to Sunnie. "Guess that says a lot. Let's go inside."

She led the way through a side door that opened by way of a combination lock. A combination she conveniently knew.

As they entered the building, Cisco noticed a few more signs of life and was glad for a little warmth. From somewhere unseen came a low bass voice, mumbling in a tone that sounded a lot like chanting. Smells of coffee, eggs and bacon wafted along the corridors and competed with the normal smells associated with medical offices.

Sunnie ushered him into an tiny examining room. "Wait here. I'll let the doctor know we've arrived."

He leaned against the examining table and tried to clear his head. Would Sunnie be back or would she disappear? He knew he should be on guard, but his mind swirled with more intimate questions about the tiny, sad-eyed woman called Sunnie. A woman who knew how to throw a grown man and who could make a terrific shot with a sniper's rifle.

Many miles away from the medical clinic, in a mansion perched high on a cliff overlooking the San Juan River, the man who was known as the Navajo Wolf was fighting his own medical problems. All his power and money could not stop the effects of a thousand years of legend and magic.

Fighting an hour-by-hour battle to breathe and also to locate the parchments that could save his life, the Wolf had recently taken to staying hidden away in his house. The numbers in his army were slowly dwindling, leaving him vulnerable. But he still had many left who were loyal.

Oh, he knew that the best and the brightest of them were planning a power takeover. He was not stupid, even though the Skinwalker sickness had taken its toll on his mind. But so far he still had control. And every moment counted.

He summoned the man who could take the form of the Burrowing Owl. His closest advisor, the Owl was leading the Skinwalker's search for the parchments.

"What have you uncovered, Owl?" the Wolf asked

with a wheeze. Breathing had become more than uncomfortable, talking next to impossible.

"I'm certain today we will reach the proper underwater cave," the Owl whispered. "We're mere minutes away from having the parchments in our hands. Then it will be a minor matter of deciphering the ancient writings. We are very close."

"You had better be," the Wolf said with a grimace.

"There is another matter that needs to be taken care of," the Owl said hesitantly. "You know I don't like diverting even one man from the search, but this seems…important to follow up."

"What is it?" Irritation crawled up the Wolf's spine, but he tried to stay calm and draw out each breath. It did him no good to fly into a rage. That would only speed up his body's deterioration.

"One of your young recruits, in his human form, was sent to gather intelligence off Navajoland."

"Yes, yes. I remember agreeing to that order. What has he found?"

"There was a man, a stranger, asking questions at a bar in Farmington last night."

"What kind of questions?"

"Questions about deaths on the reservation. He seemed particularly interested in long-ago murders."

"How long-ago?" The Wolf tried to remain calm so he could focus. He knew there was some reason he was nervous about such questions. But through the fog in his mind, he couldn't reach out and grasp the memories.

"Around fifteen years ago. The time when you were gathering your new army."

"Where is this stranger? Did our man bring him?"

"That's the real problem," the Owl admitted. "The stranger agreed to follow our man. If we'd gotten him here, we would already have his mind in our control and have our answers, but…"

"What happened?"

"This stranger is tough and bright. Carries concealed weapons and seems afraid of no one. He insisted on following our man in his own car.

"As the two vehicles rounded the bend at Hawk's Way Bluff," the Owl continued, "the car had an accident and ran off the road. By the time our man realized he wasn't being followed anymore and went back, the stranger disappeared."

"I don't like the sound of this. What did our man find at the car?"

The Owl shrugged. "A second set of tracks were made by a smaller man, much shorter than five foot six. There was a small scuffle. Maybe the second man got the drop on the stranger and forced him away at gunpoint. There was a bullet hole in the side window and blood all over the front seats."

"I know of no small-size men in the Brotherhood," the Wolf said through whistling breath. "Yet I can't help but think they are somehow involved."

"We retrieved the stranger's laptop from his disabled sedan," the Owl added as an afterthought. "I was sure we'd have the answers we seek from that machine by now, but apparently this stranger encodes his notes. We will have to break the code first."

A rage took hold of the Wolf. It blinded him with

fury and left him shaking. "The parchments come first," he growled.

The Wolf grabbed the Owl around the neck and squeezed until the man's eyes bugged out. "For all we know, this shooting was a Brotherhood diversion. They must realize we are closer to getting the answers than they are.

"Spend no time away from working on the parchments to decode the stranger's notes. I must have my answers first."

Sunnie flipped her cell phone closed and released her first easy breath since taking that mistaken shot in the dark. She leaned against the wall in the empty clinic hallway and wondered how long Cisco would be in Radiology. He'd been gone quite a while already.

Earlier, after Cisco had been taken from the examining room wearing nothing but a hospital gown, Sunnie had snuck into his jeans and found a wallet. She'd located his California driver's license and an ID issued by the federal U.S. Marshal's office to carry concealed weapons. That small bit of information made her more curious than ever about the dangerous, dark-eyed stranger. She'd thought about searching for a gun but hadn't had the time. It didn't matter. She really didn't care if he carried a weapon or not. Not as long as she had the rifle.

"What the hell were you thinking, April Henry?" Her old friend and distant clan cousin Dr. Ben Wauneka suddenly appeared behind her and pulled her out of the hallway and into a vacant room.

She didn't answer him, but stared up into his soft, concerned eyes with a silent challenge.

"Sorry," Ben said contritely. "I meant to call you Sunnie. The name change is hard for those of us who've known you for years.

"But it doesn't change the intent of the question," he continued with a scowl. "When you agreed to go into hiding, you swore you would not endanger yourself or anyone else by doing anything crazy."

"I've kept to myself, did what I promised. Except for that one time…" Sunnie couldn't bring herself to speak of the horrible tragedy that had brought her out of hiding and changed her entire life for the second time six months ago.

Ben's eyes clouded over at her near mention of the tragic events of six months ago. "That was our mistake—the Brotherhood's. We took too much for granted. But I'm talking about now, and you know it.

"Whatever possessed you to go out into the desert in the middle of the night with a rifle?" His eyes cleared of sadness and then filled again with questions and betrayal. "Where the hell did you even get a rifle, anyway? And for you to shoot at a perfect stranger— what has come over you? Such things are out of line with the teachings of the Navajo Way. They're…"

She took a step away and interrupted him. "Yeah, I know. Ideas like that are aligned with Navajo witches. With the Skinwalker Way."

Turning her back on him, Sunnie fisted her hands and inhaled deeply before she mistakenly made a few remarks that would cause the both of them nothing but more regret.

"I don't care," she finally said over her shoulder. "I almost had him, the Navajo Wolf. And I will yet. Getting that bastard is all I live for now. When he's gone—out of the picture for good—I don't care what becomes of me."

"Oh, my young friend." Ben put a hand on her shoulder and turned her to face him. "You know getting rid of the Wolf is the job of the Brotherhood. What good would it be for the People to defeat the evil ones at the cost of our own spirits? The Brotherhood works within Navajo tradition in order to maintain balance and harmony."

She frowned and felt her lips narrow in disapproval.

"You think we work too slow?" he asked with a small, sad smile. "An assassination won't end the terror. There are three Skinwalker lieutenants who are ready to take over for the Wolf. The ending of his life will not win the final battle with the Skinwalkers. But I promise the Brotherhood is close to having the answers. Trust in us. Don't do something like this to yourself."

The sorrow in Ben's eyes twisted in her chest. "Let me help you once more," he added in a whisper. "I'll call my wife. You know Tory will take you in without a second's hesitation. You are very important to her…to all of us."

Ben's wife was also a physician and had once been Sunnie's coworker and good friend. A few years ago Tory had come here as a brand-new Anglo medical doctor, sent to the rez to work off her school loans. The Skinwalker war had changed her life as it had changed Sunnie's. As it had changed *everything*.

"Tory is busy," Sunnie argued. "She's got her hands full being the New Plant Tender, finding the plants and herbs for you medicine men and also acting as a part-time doctor when needed. You can't expect her to drop everything to babysit me while I go through another of your cures.

"Besides, I know what I'm doing," Sunnie added forcefully. "My head is perfectly clear. I don't need anyone's help."

"We Dine need our clans and family. It's the way we were raised. It's who we are as Navajos."

Her anger came swift and hard. It replaced the warm feelings she'd always felt toward Ben and the Brotherhood.

"I have no immediate family left on the rez, as you know."

"Sunnie," Ben began again, more softly this time. "I'm of the Big Medicine Clan. The same as you. That makes me your family. It makes most of the Brotherhood your family, too. You can't turn your back on our teachings and traditions. If you do, all will really be lost. The Navajo Wolf will have won for sure."

"I will do what I have to do."

Ben shook his head with force. "No. Go back into hiding. Back to your temporary life."

"The Skinwalkers are no longer looking for me." She tried to reason with Ben. "Not since they tricked me and…left me for dead six months ago. They have no clue I'm not gone for good. You held a memorial for me and put my box in the ground. The Skinwalkers can't possibly know I'm still alive and want to hurt them."

"The Brotherhood needs things to stay that way for the time being, Sunnie. Tell you what—"

A buzz from Ben's pager interrupted him. He pulled it off the holster at his waist and stared at the message.

"Your guy Santiago is back in the examining room now," he told her as he replaced his pager. "His X-rays are waiting for me."

Ben stared at her for a second. "As usual, we're short-handed. I've used a special herbal salve on his wound, one my wife designed that cures quickly. But would you go make sure the dressings over Santiago's sutures are sufficient to hold him for a few days? I'll be there as soon as I can."

Sunnie nodded but clamped down on any further response. She didn't care what Ben or the Brotherhood thought of her anymore. It was her life, such as it was, and she was determined to do the right thing. And the right thing for her—for everyone—was getting rid of the Wolf. After that, the whole world could stop going around, for all she cared.

"Keep Santiago company until I get there," Ben told her. "Then you and I need to finish this conversation."

Sunnie moved past Ben and out of the room without another word. Her flash of irritation cooled. Despite Ben's persuasive arguments to stay out of it, the cold and calculating sniper was back and determined to finish the job she'd started before her worthless life was over.

Walking down the hall to check on Cisco brought another thought to her mind. What did he know of the Skinwalkers and the Wolf? Why had he been following them and could he lead her to the Wolf again?

She came to a decision. Those were answers she *would* have. Cisco Santiago was not leaving her sight until she had them.

Cisco tucked his T-shirt into his jeans. He'd promised to wait for the doctor, but he had no intention of doing it without his clothes. Checking on the stiletto in its secret compartment in his boot and then on the .38 he'd hidden in his leather jacket, Cisco was relieved to be fully dressed and armed once again.

His head had quit hurting when the doctor had deadened the wound in order to sew it up with a few sutures. Plus, Cisco had swallowed a couple of painkillers a while ago. There didn't seem to be much need to stick around this clinic. He still had plenty of questions, though, and he had no intention of going anywhere without answers.

A soft knock on the closed door came, and a second later it opened as Sunnie slid inside. "Oh. You're dressed already. But Dr. Wauneka is still checking your X rays. We should wait for him to make sure everything's okay."

"Everything is okay—considering that you shot me."

Her chin jutted just a fraction. But her wide eyes clouded over with obvious guilt. "It was an accident. You weren't the target."

"I figured that. So who should be here in my place?"

She gave a noncommittal shrug of one shoulder as an answer. "It's a long story. You're not Dineh, so I think I'll save my breath."

"Dineh. That's Navajo, right? So because I'm an

outsider I can't understand your motivations for wanting to kill someone? Must be an interesting culture."

Sunnie's expression was edged with surprise, but in a second her eyes narrowed down to hard, cold slits. Who was this tough woman?

He'd memorized her complete physical description in about thirty seconds under these florescent lights. She was five-three without the boots. Five-four or -five with them. Weight one hundred even—or close. Her thick, dark brown hair had been pulled back in an untidy ponytail. She had intelligent amber-colored eyes and fine copper-colored skin. Her slender body was in excellent condition, with muscular calves and strong shoulders. The overall picture was starkly beautiful, but that didn't tell him a thing about the woman inside.

"I need to check the dressing on your wound," she said as her eyes turned sad. "Sit down in that chair, please."

It was the bleak look that captured his attention and caused him to lose focus. He did as she requested but never took his gaze from her expressive face.

"How old are you?" he asked without thinking.

"None of your business."

"Your eyes say early thirties, but your skin and body seem to say more like early twenties."

Standing beside him, she bent and gently tugged on the bandages. "This needs a little more tape. Hold it." Going to the cabinet, she turned her back on him so he could no longer see her eyes.

"I'd put my money somewhere in between. Twenty-eight?"

"Decent guess." She turned and, with a clash of her

gaze against his, began fiddling with the dressing on his forehead once again. "Sit still."

"I thought you were a waitress. What does bandaging a wound have to do with that?"

"I'm only helping out. The clinic is short on staff."

That wasn't much of an answer. In fact, she hadn't given him a decent response to even one question yet. But he *would* have the answers. She owed him that much.

The Navajo doctor entered the room. "Mr. Santiago, it looks like you have a concussion. The cut on your forehead will heal quickly—a few days and you'll never notice it. But the concussion needs watching."

"I'll be fine."

The doctor checked Sunnie's work with the bandage and nodded his head in approval. Then he turned his attention back to Cisco. "I have no doubt you will be fine. But I wish we had a room for you here. Rest, plenty of fluids and ice packs on that goose egg are my prescription. Do you have family or friends nearby who can look after you?"

"No. But—"

"I'll do it," Sunnie volunteered, surprising Cisco. Her words said one thing, mirroring his intent, but he could swear her eyes were still shooting bullets in his direction, saying the exact opposite. Was it only guilt?

"That isn't wise," the doctor told her with a scowl. "You said you were going back to…work. You can't do that and keep an eye on him, too."

"I never said I was going back to *work,*" Sunnie said as she glowered at the doctor. "I'm on vacation for a few days. He should be fine in forty-eight hours. Right?"

Something was going on here that was making Cisco more curious than ever. These two seemed to be close, yet they obviously were in disagreement about something important. Watching her interact with this Navajo doctor made Cisco wonder if she might have a split personality.

Things were not adding up.

So he made a snap decision.

Chapter 3

Curiosity was killing him. His honed instincts were quivering. Whatever was going down here would end up being something he had to know in order to find his father's murderer. That was the whole point of his being on the rez. Plain common sense told him that getting shot while following a lead could not be coincidence.

He needed Sunnie for the answers. And, by God, he was sticking close until she coughed them up.

"I'd be grateful to you for helping out," he told her before turning back to the doctor. "If it's only for a day or two, I shouldn't be much trouble. She seems competent enough, and you said I need to be watched. Why not her?"

The doctor didn't seem happy about the turn of events. Cisco didn't care. These people hadn't done a whole lot for him up to now. But they would.

With obvious hesitation the doctor said, "All right. If you don't mind being helped by the same woman who shot you, she's capable. But eat lightly for today. Remember to get rest and fluids." He turned then to talk to Sunnie with a furious look that didn't make sense to Cisco. "Stay inside as much as possible. It'll be safer that way."

Cisco thought that a strange kind of order. But he had another pressing question he needed to ask, so he let it go.

"Are the cops on the way? When I called 911, they said they'd send someone over."

"Investigator Hunter Long from the Tribal Police is waiting in my office. You can stop in and give him a statement before you go. *Both* of you."

Many miles from Raven Wash Clinic and just across the San Juan River, the Skinwalker known as the Owl was giving secret instructions to one of the Skinwalker lieutenants loyal only to him. "I want to know where that stranger has gone. We've learned he is the owner of a skip-tracing firm in Los Angles, but that doesn't tell us what he's doing on the rez.

"I want him here," the Owl continued irritably, "where I can interrogate him with all our resources. Go watch his car. It's expensive. He won't leave it for long. Find out who comes for it and then follow them. The car will eventually lead you to the man."

The lieutenant had his orders and went off to follow them, leaving the Owl to worry about the stranger's true intentions. Was he an undercover operative for some law enforcement agency? If so, the Skinwalkers might be in real trouble. It was bad enough that the

Brotherhood had foiled most of their attempts at grabbing immortality. The Wolf was rich, but his power was quickly draining away.

The Owl was determined to be the next leader. But he had to make sure that when the time was right, there was an army left to lead.

Sunnie and Cisco were seated together on a couch in Ben's office, sipping hot coffee and listening as Officer Hunter Long questioned Cisco's statements. No one would mention it to Cisco, but Hunter was a member of the Brotherhood. Sunnie had called Hunter earlier, after she'd stolen a look at Cisco's ID, and told him about the shooting.

"So you're a bounty hunter, Mr. Santiago." Hunter repeated Cisco's words but shook his head. "Still, we don't know what purpose a bounty hunter would have on the rez. The Navajo police haven't received any alerts on wanted men in the area. You want to tell us why you're here?"

"I own a skip-tracing firm, yes. But I'm not here on business. I'm visiting Navajoland on a private matter." He sounded angry, irritated, for no good reason Sunnie could see. But something was bothering the man.

"You told Dr. Wauneka that you have no family or friends on the rez. So are you saying you've come alone to the Navajo reservation on a vacation?"

Sunnie watched as Cisco squirmed in his seat and averted his eyes. Her best guess was that something had just been said that wasn't truthful. Did he have friends or family on the reservation he had failed to mention? If so, why?

She would've pegged the guy as some kind of cop. But a bounty hunter better fit the tough face and hard-eyed stares. She'd seen a lot of tough faces in the last few years, but this was the first one she would've been drawn to in a kinder, gentler time.

She'd taken the opportunity to really look in his eyes while she'd worked on his bandage. Those eyes that oozed sensuality. Brown streaks mixed in with gray that at times seemed to turn to smoke. She'd be willing to wager this guy had no trouble getting women to do whatever he wanted.

Most women. But not her. All she wanted from him was the truth.

"Look," Cisco said with annoyance ringing in his voice. "Why am I being interrogated? I was the victim. This woman said she shot me in cold blood. And I've never laid eyes on her before this morning. Why aren't you talking to her?"

Hunter handed the wallet back to Cisco. "I've already spoken with Sunnie. She claims it was an accident, and since you've just admitted the two of you have no previous connection, I tend to believe her.

"I was only curious about why a man with no obvious mission would be driving around the remote Navajo desert after midnight."

Cisco slammed down his coffee mug and folded his arms over his chest. "None of your business."

Hunter's eyebrows went up, but Sunnie could see he'd hit a brick wall with the man's motives.

"Fine," Hunter said with a shake of his head. "But I'm

going to give you my card. Call my cell phone if you change your mind and want to talk about…anything."

He handed a reluctant Cisco the card. "As for the shooting, do you wish to press charges against Ms. Begay?"

Sunnie saw a muscle in Cisco's jaw twitch. "Since she's promised Dr. Wauneka she'd watch over me while I convalesce, I figure that should be punishment enough. No charges need to be filed.

"But I want to know the extent of damage to my car," he added. "Can you give me the number of a towing service? I need to call my insurance company."

"A local garage was called when you first came into the clinic. Mechanic named Junior Gashie towed it in. You can check with him as soon as we're done here."

Sunnie hadn't much liked Cisco's answer about the charges. The man had something in mind where she was concerned; Sunnie could feel his cloaked motives like a worm crawling under her skin.

But then, she'd promised to get her own answers. So she would deal with Mr. Santiago and whatever he had in mind all by herself. Later.

Cisco nodded his head, and Hunter turned to address her. "This isn't totally over for you. After Mr. Santiago has recuperated, you and I will have another chat. For now, I just want that rifle."

"What?"

"I'm confiscating the weapon, Sunnie. Turn it over."

Her rifle? The one thing that had come to mean the most to her over the last six months? No way.

"Come on. Where is it?"

Folding her own arms over her chest in a mimicked move of Cisco's earlier one, she narrowed her lips in a thin frown. She wouldn't tell Hunter no, but he'd have to drag the location out of her.

"It's in her Jeep," Cisco volunteered. "In the locker box behind the seats. I made her lock it up before we entered the clinic."

She spun on him. "Gee, thanks a lot."

Hunter chuckled. "Yeah, I see where the two of you together is going to be a whole lot worse than jail time. Good luck with that."

Oh, yeah. She would definitely deal with Mr. Cisco Santiago. Now she simply couldn't wait.

Hell. Cisco tried to control his irritation. The shock of having to accommodate questions from one of the two men he'd promised himself to avoid at all costs still fueled the anger rushing through his veins. He'd had to use tremendous restraint just to stay quiet.

But in his own defense, it had been a blow looking into the face of a man who was supposed to be a stranger and seeing familiar gray eyes staring out at him. The anger had come up in his throat, fast and strong. Had Hunter Long been anyone else, any other cop, Cisco might've been more willing to talk to him.

As it was, the Rockies would have to move to the East Coast before Cisco allowed himself to be hooked into such a ridiculous situation. Imagine having to see his own half brother looking at him like the complete stranger he was. The whole thing had hurt, knowing the truth, and he wasn't likely to repeat the experience.

Cisco flicked surreptitious glances at Sunnie as she drove them to the garage to check on his car. His initial impression of her, sitting in the driver's seat, had been of a bleak and calculating woman.

The first thing she'd done when they'd left the clinic was flip on large aviator shades that almost covered her whole face. They completed the perfect image of a stark professional killer. A woman who could stalk another human being without remorse. But he knew what her eyes were like under those dark glasses. Warm and sensual sometimes, sad and frightened at others. The haunted look in them was going to stick with him forever.

Still, she *had* been stalking someone out in the desert last night. He knew it. His half brother—Hunter Long the cop—knew it. And Ben Wauneka, the doctor, knew it, too.

Cisco just needed to figure out who the target had been. And to understand why, even after she'd shot him, he felt safer with her than he had since he'd entered the rez.

She slowed the Jeep, and the question came out of his mouth before he gave it a second thought. "Is Sunnie your real name?"

"Wh-what?"

"I mean, well, your disposition is not exactly what I'd call full of sweetness and light. Not with those dark looks and deep frowns."

"Sunnie is the nickname I was given as a kid," she said with a tilt of her head. "My maternal uncle gave it to me long ago. It's what I go by now."

"What's your real name?"

Not answering, she pulled up outside a place with a sign that said Junior's Paint and Body Shop and parked.

"Looks like they're getting ready to close. Your sedan is probably locked up for the night."

Before unbuckling, he reached over and clamped down on her wrist. "I will find out, *mija*. That and everything else, too. I don't give up so easily."

She sniffed and ripped her arm from his grip.

They went inside the office and found the owner closing up. Sunnie introduced them, and Cisco got the feeling that here was another Navajo who was not thrilled to see her hanging out with a stranger like himself. So far, at least three of the locals seemed to know her well, shared some secret with her, but were not at all happy about seeing her.

After he paid the garage guy a deposit on the repairs and called his insurance adjuster, Cisco talked his way into the fenced backyard so he could get his stuff out of the Charger.

"Well, the damage doesn't look too bad," Sunnie said when they came close.

He wasn't willing to concede that yet. The daylight was rapidly waning and shadows covered everything on the east side of the garage.

After a moment's inspection, he found the side window was busted out and the front bumper damaged, but other than that the car really didn't appear to be in too bad a shape. It could've been a lot worse.

Junior, the garage owner, had told him they'd found the car with the keys still in the ignition. With them in hand, Cisco headed for the trunk.

It took him seconds to see that his laptop had been stolen. Hell. Double hell. The thieves could be anyone. Tow truck driver. Cops. Anyone.

Thank goodness his notes had been encrypted. Losing them was the real tragedy, but no use crying over their loss now.

"What's the matter?"

Cisco turned at the sound of Sunnie's voice. She was staring down into the trunk with her hands on her hips.

"Someone bagged themselves free electronics at my expense."

"You've been robbed?"

"Looks that way."

"We'll notify the police. But I can guarantee you right now that none of Junior's people had anything to do with it."

Turning to check over her shoulder, she appeared to be a woman who was worried about something—or someone. "We need to leave so Junior can go home before dark. Let's take your duffel and get out of here."

Nodding his agreement, he waited until she leaned away and then covertly reached under the driver's seat to grab his spare cuffs. They went easily into his pocket. Sunnie was definitely not going to sneak away from him before she answered a few questions honestly for once—even if he had to chain her to him to prevent it.

He slammed the passenger door and turned back to help with his duffel. But he found the view of her bending over the trunk to work his duffel free so hypnotic that he could only stand there for a second and watch. Treated to a first-class glance of a firm female bottom clad in tight jeans, he began to revise his opinion of the woman who'd shot him. She wasn't looking so stark at the moment.

Pulling the duffel free of the trunk, she turned to face

him. Then he really looked again. A lush, sensual mouth turned up at the corners when she caught him staring.

"You going to keep on standing there?" she asked with a roll of her eyes. "Let's move."

A small smile crept over her lips and Cisco's body reacted. She was tough but sexy as hell, and he'd never been quite so turned on so fast by anyone in his life.

His pent-up anger vanished in that instant, replaced by more questions and an irrational need to protect her.

Crap. He'd be a lot better off getting his head together and finding his edge again. She had answers. That's all he wanted from her.

Taking her job as nursemaid seriously, Sunnie made sure Cisco was buckled in, then stepped on the gas and took off on the backstreets of Shiprock. Her nerves were shot to hell. Something didn't feel right.

"Where are we headed?" he asked.

"I have a small apartment. But it's on the other side of the rez. Maybe two and half hours from here. I've got a computer setup that you can probably make do if you need to check e-mail. And I know you'll get the rest you need there, too. You mind the long ride?"

"Whatever. I'm fine." He was staring at her profile in the flaming glow of the setting sun and making her more nervous than ever. "What about you?"

"What do you mean?"

"You look pale. Want me to drive?"

She couldn't help the nervous laugh. "Let's wait until we get out of town at least."

Her unease increased as they drove farther away from

the garage. What was going on around Shiprock on this late afternoon that seemed so different? She couldn't see anything wrong. But something was.

One of the things about Shiprock she hated the most was the fact there were only two main roads leading out of town. The main route of Navajo Route 666, now U.S. 491, going north and south. And the two-lane Route 64 going east and west.

Both highways were far too wide-open, too exposed. Remembering her promise to Ben that she would keep them out of sight, Sunnie racked her brain for alternate routes. She'd been raised near here and knew the short-cuts, but there simply wasn't any way around it—for at least a few miles they would have to drive on one of the main roads.

But they couldn't afford to be spotted.

She found herself holding her breath as they drove south on 491. At this time of day, the view of the monolith called Shiprock was framed in crimsons and magentas from the western sun, setting abruptly in the desert. Whenever she passed this way at sunset, the sight always made her catch her breath.

This time fear trapped the air in her lungs. She put her foot down harder on the gas pedal and hoped she wouldn't be stopped by one of the two traffic lights in town.

Sliding through the main intersection on a yellow light, she took a breath. And then she heard it. Clearly.

The buzz of the Skinwalkers.

Right here at the edge of town? Oh, man.

On pure instinct, she reached over and shoved hard at Cisco's back. "Get down!"

"What the hell?"

"Try to stay out of sight." Checking her rearview mirror, she spotted a huge SUV on their trail.

She downshifted the Jeep and floored it. The whine of the transmission competed with the buzzing in her ears as she shot down the nearly empty highway.

Damn, damn, damn. Where could they go to get away?

"Mind telling me what the hell you're doing?" Cisco asked with a snarl in his voice.

"Trying to save our butts," she yelled over the screaming engine and the wailing wind.

Up ahead on the two-lane part of the highway she saw a short line of cars also going south. Traffic must've recently been stopped by the red light back in Shiprock. Maybe those cars could be her answer.

She roared up behind the last car in the line, took a breath and crossed the double yellow line to pass. It took guts, but she managed to force her way back in between the last car and the poky one in front of it.

"That's enough. I've had it. Pull over," Cisco shouted. "You're crazy. I'm driving."

Sunnie shook her head. "Not yet."

Something had to give. She could still see the headlights of the tall SUV lumbering behind them menacingly and bringing up the rear of their line of cars.

Putting every bit of her currently shaky intelligence to work, she tried to figure a way out. She knew Dead Man's Wash was a few miles up ahead and decided it was a chance she would have to take.

If only they could get a little lucky.

Praying that the SUV wouldn't play the same game

of chicken as she was, Sunnie wished for a lot more traffic, only this time coming from the other direction. When the sign for the upcoming bridge over the wash appeared, she also saw the break she'd been hoping for.

A long line of headlights was coming toward them. She couldn't wait for a better opportunity. Flooring the old Jeep once again, she passed a couple more cars, barely making it back into her lane before the oncoming cars thundered alongside them, traveling in the opposite direction. Thanking the *Yei,* she was grateful to have put a few more vehicles between her Jeep and the SUV.

Hitching her breath, she slowed and waited for the opposite line of cars to cross the bridge that spanned the dry wash. The minute her Jeep was across and the last car in the oncoming line of traffic had passed, she turned the wheel hard to the left and zipped across the other lane. She held on as the Jeep bounced off the highway and down into the desert on the far side of the bridge. Slamming on the brakes as she felt the sand beneath her tires, she fought the steering wheel.

The ride was rough, through poisonweed and sagebrush, and she glanced over to check on Cisco. But it was too dark to see him clearly. She twisted the wheel left once again as they flew down the embankment and into the dry wash under the bridge.

Praying her sudden maneuver had been hidden from behind by the line of cars going the opposite direction, she stood on the brake pedal and doused the lights.

"You *are* nuts," Cisco growled. "I swear…"

"Shush. Quiet."

His deadly silence told her how he felt about things.

Her mind whirled, filling with useless thoughts and adrenaline rushes. She'd wait ten minutes and then double back. There was a way off the highway a few miles back that would take them in the other direction and give them time to disappear.

"Tell me what this is all about," he muttered.

"Not now."

"Sunnie…"

"I told you—I'm saving your ass."

"From who?"

Her shaky nerves finally got to her. She couldn't help the sudden frustration and irritation. She'd saved his damned life. Shouldn't that count for something?

Sunnie turned to look at him in the starlight as words spilled out of her mouth. "From the Skinwalkers, dammit. Now shut up and be still before we both end up dead."

Chapter 4

Cisco sat in stony silence, intent on watching her while they drove out of the wash. They'd apparently lost the SUV, at least temporarily. But had she really said what he thought he'd heard?

Skinwalkers? He'd done a little research on the Navajo before he'd made this trip and knew Skinwalkers were supposedly evil Navajo men who dealt in witchcraft and who could change their form into animal shapes. Is that what she was talking about?

Similar tales of black witchcraft had been spun by his old Mexican grandmother. His *abuela* claimed to have actually seen animals change form. The stories she'd told seemed so real he'd ended up half believing in them. But, then again, maybe he had been as crazy as his grandmother.

Maybe Sunnie *was* crazy. Maybe that's why none of the locals they'd met had been thrilled to see her. But if she were nuts, surely that Navajo doctor would have found a way to warn him. Right?

"Where are we going?" he asked as she pulled the four-wheel-drive Jeep off the sand and onto the highway.

"There's a local road, not well marked and not as far back as Shiprock city limits. It'll take us in the opposite direction from my apartment, east off the reservation. It ends up in the outskirts of Farmington. I'm hoping we can get lost in city traffic."

"Farmington isn't much of a bustling city."

She gave a slight shrug. "I doubt they'll follow us off the reservation even if they manage to spot us leaving."

He wanted to shout that he couldn't help her if he didn't know everything. "What'll we do in Farmington? Notify the police?"

Shooting him a dark glance, she shook her head. "You can call Hunter if you want, but neither the Farmington Police nor the San Juan County Sheriff will be able to help us any. This trouble is strictly a Navajo problem."

There was no shot in hell of him calling Hunter Long. "But you think that SUV was following us because of me. Why? I'm not Navajo." At least he didn't think he had any Navajo blood. Though at this point in his life he wasn't too sure of the complete details of his background.

In the glow of headlights from oncoming cars he spotted her setting that pretty little jaw. "Duh," she ground out. "You could've fooled me. But you've managed to wade into a big freakin' Dine problem all the same, haven't you?"

"I'm not getting this. How come you're so sure the guys who were following us weren't after you?"

"Because they don't know I exist."

Hunter gave himself a mental shake. Why bother to talk to her at all? She never gave him a straight answer.

But life was what you made of it. And he had vowed to make her tell him the whole story before they were done.

Just not right now. His head was pounding, his vision blurred and fuzzy. He needed to get inside and out of the wind before he made any further attempts at getting her to talk. Cisco couldn't think of a way under her defenses until he rested.

"You're the driver," he said grudgingly. "So drive on. But I'll need someplace to lie down soon."

She flicked him a worried glance and nodded her head. "I know an out-of-the-way place, an old motel on the far side of Farmington. Twenty more minutes. Can you make it?"

Oh, he'd make it, all right. And when he did, and after he'd caught a short nap, the next sound he would hear would be her spilling secrets about what had been happening and why he was stuck in the middle. She wouldn't maneuver around talking then.

Grateful for the peace and quiet, Sunnie sat on the rim of a rusted tub in the tiny bathroom of the motel room she'd rented for cash, considering her new opinions on the subject of trust. Once upon a time, she'd trusted everyone. But as of six months ago, she'd gone through a complete transformation and no longer trusted anyone. Not people she'd known all of her life and certainly not strangers.

The stranger asleep on the bed in the next room was injured and needed her nursing help for a while. But she couldn't find any valid reason to trust him.

When the Skinwalker SUV had caught up to them so easily after they'd left Junior's, she'd been positive Cisco had somehow signaled them. Now she wasn't so sure. He had been completely surprised when she'd mentioned the Skinwalkers. Really at a loss as to what she'd meant. She'd seen it in his expression.

His shock had dulled her edge of fear. In the beginning Sunnie hadn't cared if Cisco turned out to be one of the bad guys. Or even if he'd been sent to finish the job and murder her. Her life was not the point.

The point was to kill the Wolf. And she was determined to live long enough to see the bastard dead. Then it simply didn't matter.

Bending to riffle through Cisco's duffel, she contemplated her odd but automatic reactions to the man. Perhaps, as she'd helped him out of his coat and boots and onto the double bed, she'd lingered over the musky scent of him just a little too long. And just maybe she'd relished combing his deep brown and mink-soft hair off his forehead a little too much. Maybe.

But the thick stubble on the carved angles of his face had been fascinating. The men she'd known well in her life—her fiancé and her family—none of them had had much in the way of facial hair. The mysterious shadow was what made Cisco look so dangerous. Perhaps that was why she got an electric sizzle whenever he looked her way.

Thinking about his watchful gaze for a moment, she remembered the disdain in those intelligent ebony-colored eyes when the two of them were being questioned by Hunter back at the clinic. Clearly Cisco hadn't cared for Hunter Long. The unknown reasons for his animosity toward a tribal policeman made her curious.

Some of his words also sounded as though he hadn't cared much for her, either. But his gazes told a whole different story.

In the bright florescent lights he'd studied her with a blatant physical assessment. She might be naive to many of the sensual ways of men and women, but those looks had most definitely been sexual as they'd slid down her body. Her nipples had even tightened in response. Which in turn had caused a myriad of strange feelings to swim inside her. But they also gave the first clue that she was actually lusting after a complete and potentially dangerous stranger.

Returning her attention to his duffel, Sunnie ran her hands under the folded underwear and extra pair of jeans and tees. First she came across a loaded magazine, buried under shaving cream and deodorant. The bullets and the fit seemed right for a handgun the size of about a .38. That made her remember the "concealed" weapon she hadn't thought of since they'd been at the clinic. Did he still have one on him?

She wasn't afraid. But she didn't like the idea of him being armed when she wasn't.

Hurrying through the rest of his duffel, she came up with only one other interesting thing—a small manila envelope containing old news clippings. They were from the local Navajo newspaper, dated about fifteen years ago. She didn't take the time to study them carefully, but all of them concerned a body that had been found in a burned-out car on the reservation.

Interesting. Almost familiar. But she had a more pressing problem at the moment. She needed to find that gun before Cisco woke up and once again had the upper hand.

Cisco awoke with a start. What was that noise and why had it brought him up from a sound sleep? It took him a second to orient himself to his surroundings. Oh, yeah. He was in the cheap motel room Sunnie had rented.

Sunnie. He shot a glance around the darkened room and past the open doorway into the small lighted bath. Easy to see Sunnie was among the missing. Damn. Had she left him asleep and gone for good?

Again he heard the same noise that must've awoken him. Only this time he knew what he'd been hearing. The door to the outside parking lot rattled lightly. Someone was trying to get into the room.

He exploded erect out of bed, reaching for the chair and the coat lying across it at the same time. Dipping his hand into the inside coat pocket and searching for his .38, he came up with nothing but air. What the hell? The weapon was gone. Sunnie. Dammit. She'd taken his .38 and left him without so much as a word.

Gritting his teeth and vowing to catch up to her or die trying, Cisco decided to defend himself from his immediate adversary by picking up an old standing lamp that was heavy enough to dent a man's head. He ripped the cord from the wall. With it hefted above his shoulder, he stepped to the side of the doorjamb and waited.

If nothing else, he would have surprise on his side.

The lock clicked and the doorknob turned. Not long to wait now. He tensed and bounced on the balls of his stocking-clad feet, ready to spring at whoever came through the door.

But before it opened more than an inch, he heard someone softly calling his name. "Cisco? Are you awake?"

He dropped the lamp and wrenched open the door at the sound of Sunnie's voice. He'd been the one to be surprised, but he still had an open opportunity.

Grabbing her bodily and pitching her onto the bed, he leaned over to reach in his coat pocket and came up with the handcuffs all in one move. She'd missed those.

Sunnie shrieked. The backpack and plastic sacks in her hands went flying. Before she could recover and scramble off the bed, he flung himself at her. Sitting astride her body, Cisco tussled with the tiny woman. She was a lot stronger than she looked, he thought for not the first time.

But within seconds he'd managed to subdue her enough to cuff one of her hands to the old iron bedpost. Backing off and flipping on the overhead light, he paused and stared down at her while she continued to struggle with the cuff.

What a magnificent woman, with that perfectly glorious body and majestic spirit.

Checking the curve of her breasts as her chest heaved and her breathing came in pants, Cisco found himself leering through the shadows at the shapely female waist and hips. He forced his gaze away.

What brought that on? he wondered. He might be a lot of things, but he didn't lust after a near stranger he'd just cuffed to a bed. How long since he'd had sex, anyway? A couple of months? Four? Maybe longer than that.

He'd been busy. Too busy to remember or care.

Looking at her flushed face and deadly glare, he couldn't even remember when or if he'd ever seen a woman he'd wanted more. The idea was a stunner. His body was tight with desire for someone he normally wouldn't have looked at twice.

His regular sexual partners were more the type who knew what they wanted and knew how to get it. They were sensual in a blatant way. Hot-tempered, yes, but also warm and open and happy to walk away alone in the end.

Sunnie had all this incredible physical energy. That alone made him wonder about her staying power. She also tended toward quick-tempered, and he knew that could be a turn-on at the right times. But the sudden somber and bleak looks perpetually marring her beautiful face should've left him cold. Instead he was having a difficult time not picturing her naked and responding with all that power underneath him.

"Where's the weapon? What'd you do with it?" He folded his arms and fought to keep his voice steady.

She eyed him with a suspicious but level look. "The gun? Is that why you attacked me? Jeez. You took ten years off my life. Why couldn't you just ask?"

He didn't like her avoiding the question, so he bent to pick up her backpack. "Let's see what we have in here."

Dumping the contents on the end of the bed, Cisco smiled as water bottles toppled out along with lacy thong panties, chocolate bars, a cotton T-shirt and…his .38. He checked the cylinder, then the clip, made sure it was loaded and locked. When he was satisfied, he shoved the weapon in his waistband at the hollow of his back.

"You want to tell me why you found it necessary to steal my .38?" He edged closer to her. "And why you left me here alone without a word?"

She was still panting hard from her struggles, and the sounds of her heavy breathing once again stirred something within him that he'd been trying to avoid. He would rather not notice anything physical about her at all.

"I went to buy food," she muttered. "I thought you might be hungry. And you were sleeping so soundly I didn't want to wake you."

Food? Now that she'd mentioned it, he could smell fast food. Hamburgers and French fries, if he didn't miss his guess. Checking around, he spotted the take-out sacks she'd been carrying, now strewn around the floor and on the bed.

"So you took the .38 to protect yourself in case the bad guys caught up to you while you were out there alone?"

She leaned her head back against the wall and narrowed her eyes. "Sure. Why else?"

Wisps of her long ebony hair partially obscured his view of her eyes, so he couldn't see how the falsehood affected her expression. But he heard the lie clearly in her voice.

Picking up one of the plastic sacks off the floor, he inspected the contents. Finding cold soft drinks inside, he calmly pulled out a Diet Coke, jerked open the tab and offered her the can.

"Nice of you to think of me," he said wryly.

Sunnie grabbed the can with her free hand, shoved aside the hair from her face with the back of her hand and drank deeply. She must be thirsty after their wrestling match, he thought guiltily. And not too proud or scared to accept the offer of quenching it. Good for her.

"You have a terrific way of showing appreciation," she ground out after swallowing. "How about uncuffing me?"

He bent to pick up another sack. "In a bit. Let's eat and do a little talking first." Pulling up the chair, he sat just out of her reach.

"You're keeping me cuffed? But I'm not armed. I'm no threat to you."

"You might not be armed, but you could well be a threat. I want some straight answers first."

She was shooting major nasty looks in his direction. Maybe food would help both of them.

Peeking into the bag, he found items wrapped in opaque paper. "What's this? I thought I smelled hamburgers."

"There's another sack with the hamburgers and fries. That one must be the Navajo tacos. I bought them for me."

"Tacos?"

Holding out a hand, Sunnie smirked. "Fry bread, refried beans and cheese, *Naakaii*."

Cisco handed her the sack. "What'd you just call me?"

"*Naakaii*. One of the Mexican Clan people. I thought it was only fair to call you that after you called me 'my dear' in Spanish. Clearly you have a Mexican-American heritage. That makes you *Naakaii*."

He found the bag containing hamburgers, sat back down and dug in. "Which you could've picked on by my name alone. But I'm more interested in talking about what's going on around here."

"Find someone else to talk to. And don't call me your dear again."

Dios mio but she was bright and sharp. A real handful. He'd have to watch what he said.

Sunnie blinked and tried to focus on Cisco. How had he moved fast enough to put her into this position and cuff her to the bedpost? She'd thought herself a small but quick opponent, capable of taking on men almost twice her size. It was a question of mind over matter.

Her mind must've suddenly gone blank when his body had crushed hers down on the bed. For sure, the heat and closeness had driven all matter from her head.

Staring into eyes that had turned the color of icy steel, she even managed to lose track of what was being said. The look in his eyes was suddenly suggesting he would like to trade the metal cuffs in for silken bonds. His expression had turned hot. Kinky. Tempting.

For a minute the idea made her nearly hyperventilate. Then she shook herself back to her senses. She tugged once again at her wrist, moving the locked cuff up and down on the skinny bedpost and rattling the metal.

"It would be a lot easier to eat if I could use two hands," she muttered while glaring daggers in his direction.

Cisco silently shrugged and chewed off another bite of his hamburger.

Hell. She was too hungry to sit here like a lump, so she took one more sip of Diet Coke and unwrapped a taco. Maybe she could better think of a way out of her current predicament on a full stomach.

She fumed and ate, considering the idea of trust. The guy was a jerk. Admittedly a sexy, gorgeous one, but a jerk nonetheless. Still, her gut instincts were continuing to tell her that he could be trusted, though he'd done not one thing so far to earn it.

Finishing his burger, he tossed the paper wrapping into the lopsided open trash can sitting in the corner of the room. "Let's start our discussion with Skinwalkers, shall we?" he asked smugly as he popped the few last French fries into his mouth. "You said it was Skinwalkers chasing us. You want to explain that remark?"

"Well..." she said, stalling for an idea. "According to legend, Navajo Skinwalkers are..."

"Skip the lecture, sugar. I've read up on Navajo legends. And I know something of the origin of the Wolf Clan, those evildoers in Navajo life who are capable of changing form from human to animals with superpowers. I know that the story about Monster Slayer killing many evils but skipping Greed, and then Greed finding parchments that showed him how to change form, is a tradition that's as old as the Navajo tribe.

"But I'm not buying the idea we were being followed by spooks that go bump in the night. Try again."

She was fresh out of stories and ideas. Like it or not, Cisco Santiago was going to have to accept the truth.

"You may think you know about Skinwalkers," she began. "But until you've spent enough time in our vast territory or have seen one and experienced the damage they can do, you know nothing at all."

"And you have?" he broke in. "You've seen one?"

Nodding, Sunnie tried to block the pictures of their

victims from entering her mind. The images threatened to drive her back to debilitating sadness, so she kept talking. "Unfortunately I have. What you don't know about the Skinwalkers is that a few years ago a Navajo man versed in witchcraft arose out of seemingly nowhere to form a new Skinwalker cult. He'd learned the secrets to changing over and began recruiting an army of followers.

"Once he had a big enough group gathered, he became the Navajo Wolf and trained them on how to manipulate people—to confuse and frighten the Dine. The idea being to gain power and money. His army learned their lessons well. The Skinwalkers use mind control, disease, pain and deception—the whole bag of evil tricks warned about for centuries in the Dine oral traditions."

Cisco had been studying Sunnie carefully as she'd said her piece. Over the many years of tracking people down he'd learned to read emotions and lies in a person's eyes, even when they were trying hard to disguise their thoughts.

Her eyes told a more fascinating tale than her fanciful words. At first she'd been squirming, trying to get out of the inevitable discussion. Then he'd seen the sadness overpower her. A bleak depression quickly captured her entire being as she'd given in and told her story. She believed every word she'd spoken.

There was something even more expressive behind those eyes, too. He didn't know what. Not yet.

But he was starting to believe her story. At least, he believed that *she* believed it. "So you really accept that a screwball cult is trying to control the modern Navajo nation by shape-shifting and witchcraft? Have you ever seen one of these guys changing over?"

"Not actually in the act of changing, no," she replied. "But I have certainly experienced the full fury of their animal personae. It's chilling. Deadly."

"And you're positive they drive SUVs around the reservation, trying to kill or capture strangers. You said they didn't know you exist, so I imagine you believe it's me they were chasing. Why me?"

The look in her eyes turned dark again, determined instead of sad. "I was hoping you would tell me that. Why were you following a Skinwalker vehicle out in the remote desert in the middle of the night?"

"Was I? How do you know for sure that young Navajo man in the SUV was a Skinwalker? He looked normal to me."

"Uh…"

"Might as well spill it, *mija*. It couldn't be any worse than what you've said already."

"Maybe you're right about that," she answered quietly. "There's a secret society of good medicine men in Navajoland dedicated to destroying the Skinwalkers. They call themselves the Brotherhood. Early on, the group learned that Skinwalkers emit a high-pitched buzzing sound when they're in their animal personae or when an attack is about to take place.

"That SUV you were following was buzzing louder than a swarm of killer bees. I'm surprised you didn't have to cover your ears."

Had he noticed the vibration? Perhaps he had and

shrugged it off as just another strange sound in the black desert night. Cisco sensed Sunnie truly believed everything she'd been saying about these Skinwalkers. Was he beginning to believe her stories, too?

He should ask her why she'd been out in the desert herself and, for that matter, who she'd been gunning for when she'd accidentally shot him. But there was something else, another question nagging at the back of his mind.

"Are you a member of this Brotherhood deal?"

The question brought a half smile to her lips. "Not me. They must be medicine men, shaman of the Navajo nation. No females."

"So who is a member?"

Her expression turned wary, unsure. He couldn't blame her for being reluctant to answer. For all she knew, he might be a spy for the bad guys.

Digging into his pocket, he withdrew the key to the cuffs and unlocked them. "Sorry about the cuffs. I couldn't think of any other way to pin you down. I'm not one of them—you know I'm not. I'm not even positive I believe they exist."

She rubbed her wrist and made him cringe thinking he might've hurt her. "I know you're not a Skinwalker. But I'm not sure what—or who—you are."

Cisco didn't want to talk about himself or the real reason bringing him to the reservation just yet. But he couldn't help pressing her for a little more information.

"Is Hunter Long a member of the Brotherhood?"

"Yes." She'd said it with no fanfare, no hesitation. "And Dr. Ben Wauneka and Junior Gashie, too."

"Why were you so quick to admit that? Haven't you considered the possibility of putting those men in a bad position by identifying them?"

"The Skinwalkers already know the names of most of the Brotherhood. I can't think why anyone else would care."

The unsaid questions hung in the air. *Why do you care, Bounty Hunter? What's it to you?*

Cisco silently picked up the sacks with remnants of her tacos, pitched them and the empty soda can in the trash. He wasn't going to answer those questions. At least not until he got a better handle on the situation he'd stumbled into.

And not until he had a good reason to trust in her and to fully understand those odd, sad expressions.

Chapter 5

Surprised he'd unlocked her handcuff, Sunnie suddenly felt a lot more tolerant of the man. After all, it had been her bullet that had grazed his head. He'd been chased and interrogated, and she'd taken his gun. So far, he wasn't having the greatest of days.

"You want anything else?" Cisco asked as he loomed above her. "There's another hamburger and a couple of sodas left."

She shook her head. "But you look tired. You need your rest. I'll move and give you back your bed."

Holding up a hand, palm out, he said, "I'm not crazy about the idea of waking up again and finding you and my .38 long gone. There's no way of locking the door from the inside, is there?"

"I won't leave again without waking you up. I

promise." She hopped off the bed. "I'll sit in the chair and keep an eye on you like the doctor said. I have no intention of sneaking off."

He placed a couple of fingers at his temple and rubbed, seemingly unable to hold off the grimace of obvious pain. "Are you married?"

"What? No. Why do you ask?"

"Engaged? Dating someone special?"

The questions brought back the bleakness and depression, quickly swamping her with unwanted emotions again. But over the last six months she'd learned to bury them. Quickly and efficiently.

Lifting her chin, she stared at him. She wasn't about to explain herself to this arrogant stranger. At the same time, she had already given a thought or two about his romantic status, too. Out of idle curiosity, of course.

His questions gave her the open door to ask her own. "I don't do entanglements anymore. I was engaged once. It didn't work out well. I won't go there again.

"How about you?" she added before he could disengage. "You married or otherwise entangled?"

He shook his head. "No time." Then he studied her for another second. "No real inclination, either."

As much as she was glad to learn that, she schooled her expression and her words not to let him know. "Why the questions?" He could be lying about himself, but she didn't really think so. Cisco could be a lot of things, but he didn't strike her as a liar.

"Just curious," he mumbled. "Don't want any big lug of a guy showing up to beat me to a pulp over this next suggestion."

He swiped a hand across his mouth. "How about if we sit on the bed together? We'll talk and that way we can each keep an eye on the other."

Did she dare let him get that close? "You don't trust me enough to fall asleep again?"

"About as much as you trust me, I imagine."

The two of them faced each other in an uncomfortable standoff. But as he studied her closely in that sensual, intimate way he'd done before, it was apparent she was the one sweating the silent scrutiny the most.

"You don't trust yourself, either, do you?" he asked with true insight. "Look, just sitting on the bed together doesn't mean anything. I swear I won't make any moves you don't want me to make. We'll even stay on top of the spread, fully clothed."

He was right. And then some. She trusted him *more* than she trusted herself. If he'd wanted to hurt her, he'd had ample opportunity. Plus, he needed her nursing skills for at least a few more hours.

She wanted to stay with him. Find out what he knew. There was a lot about him she wanted to learn. The guy was complicated, much more than she'd originally thought. He must have some knowledge of the Skin-walkers, even if he didn't know it. He might be able to help her get another line on the Wolf.

But she also didn't want to stay with him. Not that close, anyway. Her mouth watered at the very sight of the lean, tough body and those deep granite eyes. Could she manage to keep her head and also keep herself from giving away how much she wanted that in-your-face power hovering over her once more? Next time they wrestled, her preference would be to inflame, not subdue.

"You get comfortable," he said. "Once you're settled, I'll take the far side of the bed so you can be sure of my intentions."

Her stomach fluttered when he smiled. "It's only a double," she hedged. "Not that much room."

"Just take off your shoes and we'll see."

"Okay, I guess." This had better work out. She could not afford to get sexually involved with the man before she wrangled the information she needed. Her mind must remain focused on one goal. The one and only thing keeping her alive.

Find and kill the Navajo Wolf.

Slipping off her shoes, she sat down on the farthest corner of the bed, put one of the two skimpy pillows between her head and the wall and swung her feet around. She was fully upright and taking up the teeniest parcel of the double bed that she could manage.

Cisco chuckled as he flipped off the overhead light, leaving them in the half-light coming from the bathroom. "Hey, that sure looks cozy."

"It's fine."

He shrugged and stretched full out on the other side, with his head on the other pillow. "Okay, great."

This was all wrong. Though he wasn't lying close to her, she could feel his heat. Could smell the citrus and musk of his scent surrounding her and could swear she heard the beating of his heart.

For a few minutes she never moved a muscle, waiting for him to find a comfortable place on the bed.

Waiting for him to say he needed more room or scoot closer to her side.

But nothing happened. Not until she heard a soft snoring. When she looked over, he'd fallen sound asleep.

Must be nice. She wished she could fall asleep that fast. But for her sleep never came easily. Most of her nights were spent tossing, thinking of the past and wishing there were do-overs in life.

Sunnie stayed alert for a long time, waking him every hour or so to make sure he was okay. He seemed fine. Finally she decided to give him a few more minutes to fall back under completely and then she would slip out of bed and move to the chair. That way she could still make sure he was all right and not have to worry about disturbing him. Or about losing her resolve and sliding in closer in order to bathe in his warmth and strength.

Momentarily closing her eyes to keep from staring at his prone and very compelling body, she paid close attention to his steady breathing and was lulled by the even tones. If nothing else, he sounded healthy. By tomorrow he would probably be back to normal. Good for him. She wished she could be normal again someday, too.

But there was little chance of her ever being normal again. Her life was defined now by days, hours, minutes. She wanted her world narrowed down to only her and the evil one. Her usual trouble with falling asleep was much appreciated at the moment. It gave her more time tonight to consider a new plan.

But then, when she least expected it, Sunnie forgot her insomnia and slipped away into the dark world of dreams.

* * *

In dreams, she found herself holding a knife, not a rifle. Moonlight drifted through a shadowed forest and sent streaming rays bouncing along the steel shaft in her hand. The beams of light flashed back, blinding and dazzling her with both fear and hope.

The secrets were here, close by. She could somehow feel them beating a loud tattoo right through the bottom of her feet. Pulsating evil guarded truth, but she would overpower it. If only she could find the answers.

The growl of a beast, in harsh discord with the gentle breezes, came from somewhere nearby. She raised the knife and turned, ready to do battle. Prepared to die after finishing her mission, she calmed herself and waited for the telltale signs—the sly rustle of brush in the darkness or a glint of light against sharp fangs.

From out of nowhere the stranger came riding up on a black steed, his rifle at the ready. He stopped, turned to her with a challenging grin, both sincerity and violence shining from his gunmetal eyes.

Here was a potential partner. An answer. Perhaps hazardous to her spirit but a willing advocate for her cause. With little trepidation, she reached up and handed him the knife.

He threw back his head and laughed, then pulled her into the saddle behind him. The horse bolted and raced through the trees as the two riders adjusted themselves to working together. They charged into the shadows, while the blood beating wildly through her body gave off a sure sense of forthcoming victory.

An end was in sight. Triumph was at hand.

* * *

Cisco awoke with a start when he couldn't move his arms or legs. Somehow his limbs were restricted. Had he been drugged and tied up?

Before he could pry open his eyes, the tangy scent of woman reached his nostrils and he relaxed. Sunnie's fresh smell had already been burned into his memory. He would recognize it always.

A sure sense of her small, feminine body wrapped around his brought him wide-awake. But he didn't move a muscle, just lay there listening to her even breathing.

Light was seeping into the room around the edges of the ancient curtains that covered the lone window. Scouring a hand over his eyes to wipe away the cobwebs, he recognized the glow as sunlight and was amazed to find he'd been asleep so long.

His attention returned to the bed and his sleeping companion. Their legs were intertwined, and one of Sunnie's arms was flung across his chest. She had snuggled up close to him during the night and ended up with her nose buried in the crease of his neck.

The intimate position heated his blood and stirred awake an animal component to his personality that he needed to conquer. The urge to touch her, taste her, was strong. But he didn't do mornings. No soft rehashes of regrets and dreams for him. Especially not with a woman he had never even kissed.

Despite his many questions of trust, he'd come to the conclusion last night that he needed her. Sunnie knew her way around the reservation, understood the customs and was acquainted with many of the people. She was knowledgeable about whatever strange occurrences were going on and would be the perfect guide, a great person to use to his own ends.

Easing out from under her, Cisco decided to admire her and those useful assets from a distance. It would be safer.

Once he was standing upright, he realized his head didn't ache anymore. Lightly touching the bandage covering his sutures and feeling no pain, he smiled to himself. He was back. Strong. Ready for anything the reservation and Sunnie Begay had to throw at him.

Almost whistling at the idea of his good health, he caught himself and slipped into the bathroom instead. After he'd splashed some water on his face, there would be time enough to wake the sleeping Navajo beauty.

Wake her and talk her into accepting him as her newest best friend.

Sunnie jerked awake with heart pounding and blood boiling. Ready to defend and attack, she raised her fists, only to find Cisco bending over and shaking her by the shoulder with a big grin on his face.

"Come on, sugar. Rise and shine. Time to blow this dump and get moving."

"What?" She struggled to shake herself awake and leave the dream world behind. "Where are we going?"

He grinned again and had the nerve to sit down at the edge of the bed beside her. "Your apartment. I need to use your computer to go online. But I thought first we could find someplace closer to get a cup of coffee. You're the guide here. What do you think?"

She sat up and frowned. "I guess you're feeling better." He was too vivid. Too bigger-than-life. Too close.

"Yeah. Not a thing wrong with me."

"Hmm. You're not quite perfect. But I guess you're well enough." She'd wanted for him to be a partner, to stand beside her on her quest. Now all she wanted was more space. "It'll be a long trip around the outskirts of the rez to my place. Maybe I should drop you off at a nicer motel here in Farmington. Or down in Gallup, where it'll be safer for you to wait until Junior fixes your car. We'll find one with Internet access along with all the comforts of home."

His expression changed in an instant as he leaned in closer. "I told you once—you're not getting rid of me that easily."

She didn't flinch, but it was all she could do not to back away. Her insides tensed and adrenaline pumped.

His eyes flared, and he seemed to recognize her discomfort for what it was.

Raising a hand to her cheek, he grazed his knuckles along her jawline. "You don't want to get rid of me, do you? You want me as much as I want you. You're lying to both of us."

Blinking back her shock at his blatant touch and finding herself incapable of speech, Sunnie tried to swallow. She was bound by the spell of his gaze. Hypnotized, she froze while his fingers trailed down her throat. He narrowed the small gap between their lips. Still a millimeter away, she could feel his intensity simmering, stewing, ready to explode.

Their warm breaths mingled, became one. Two sets of

electric impulses zapped across the narrow divide while neither faded nor faltered. They both just continued staring deeply into each other's eyes, never glancing away for an instant. Time hovered just this side of fulfillment.

Finally his hand cupped the back of her neck and he lasered the inevitable kiss across her lips. Sensations of heat, fast and furious, flamed and combusted, swamping her with needs she'd never known before.

Sunnie surprised herself and moaned. He took the sound as a sign and deepened the kiss, sliding his tongue inside to duel with hers. Pressing. Demanding. She felt his other hand closing over her breast. Growing tension curled inside her, exploding in her belly.

It was suddenly too much. She couldn't breathe. The panic hit hard, right smack in the middle of her chest, as her racing heart jumped wildly.

She brought her elbow up and caught him hard in the windpipe. "No! Stop it," she demanded in a hoarse voice.

He reared back, eyes full of questions and shock as he raised his hands to defend himself. She used the opportunity, pulled away enough to put some momentum behind it and shoved at his shoulders. Overbalancing, he slipped right off the bed and hit the floor.

It took him a few gasping breaths to get a word out. During that time, Sunnie came to her senses and started feeling guilty.

"What the hell did you do that for?" he finally croaked.

She shook her head. "I don't know." But she did.

She'd let him kiss her. Touch her. Stir her needs and rob her, however momentarily, of the will and determination to finish her mission.

The lust had been there all along, of course. But she needed to be able to control it. With her own moves. Her own choices. Not his.

Cisco's wary glance drilled through her. "Well, don't do it again."

Sunnie got up and strode toward the bathroom. "Not a chance." She turned back but tried not to look directly at him. "Give me a few minutes to get myself together. Then we'll go find that coffee and head to my apartment."

"You want anything else? Just coffee?" The waitress at the Sunrise Café—all three hundred pounds of her dressed in a bubblegum-pink uniform—had taken Cisco's order and turned to Sunnie.

"No, thanks."

Cisco didn't like the overly polite tone of Sunnie's voice. She'd been quiet and reserved ever since he'd made the monumental mistake of kissing her back at the motel. The kiss itself hadn't actually been a mistake. But the yielding power of her breath mingled with his and the hot press of full breasts against his chest must've numbed his brain. Thoughts of soft lips and the firm curve of her breast in the palm of his hand made him tense and achy.

She'd kissed him back with enthusiasm *and* a sexy murmur from deep within her throat. He'd kind of lost track after that but knew the kiss had been one of the most spectacular episodes of his life.

But, then again, it had also been just plain stupid.

What had come over him? He was trying to develop a rapport between them. Instead he'd pushed her and come on like some Neanderthal.

He would have to tread lightly from here out. "You should have something to eat," he told her.

"I'm not hungry, thank you."

The waitress flipped her pad closed, rolled her eyes and walked away.

Gritting his teeth and trying not to act in his usual arrogant manner, Cisco didn't say all the right things about keeping up her strength and fueling her body. Even though he wanted to. He was determined to get some food down her, though, one way or the other.

She sipped her coffee and glared at him across the table. "So what do you usually charge?"

"Excuse me? Charge for what?"

"For finding people. What do bounty hunters get paid?"

Interesting question. This must be one of those tricky places where he would have to be extremely careful. But how could he turn it around and make her trust him?

"Bounty hunters get a percentage of the outstanding bond on a felon. Are you looking for a bail jumper?"

"Just curious. I didn't say I was looking for anyone."

"But you are, aren't you? It isn't too hard to guess you want to find whoever it was you thought you had in your sights the night you shot me by mistake."

Sunnie looked down into her cup, then checked around at the other people in the café. "You never told me what you were doing out in the desert in the middle of the night."

The two of them were sitting in an alcove, far away from any prying ears. Still, Cisco reminded himself to keep his voice low.

They might be at an impasse, but some of his answers

were already clear. She had to be hunting someone she believed to be a Skinwalker. It was now just a question of exactly who—and why.

In another gut-level decision, based somewhat on his instincts and somewhat on that spectacular kiss, he decided to tell her part of his story. Just enough to keep her interested and gain him a little more time.

"I've come to Navajoland to investigate an old murder," he told her. "That young Navajo who was leading me out into the desert said he knew someone with information. I was supposed to follow him out to a remote family's hogan to meet up with this other guy who had the answers."

Sunnie watched him with a curious expression. It was clear she was skeptical.

"I didn't realize bounty hunters investigated murders," she said. "I thought they just found criminals and returned them to jail."

"I've already mentioned this is personal."

Smiling in a wry but deliberate way, she nodded. "Yes, you did. But you didn't say why."

He wasn't ready to give up that much. Not yet.

With his continued silence, her smile turned to a frown. "I gather you had no idea the man you were following was a Skinwalker."

"No. Believe me, that thought never crossed my mind."

The expression on her face said she believed. But that didn't mean she trusted him.

The waitress appeared carrying plates of bacon, eggs and buttered toast, which she placed on the table before him. "You two need more coffee? Or anything else?"

Each of them accepted another cup of coffee but declined the offer of anything more.

Once the waitress had refilled their coffee cups and retreated, Cisco started in on his eggs. In his peripheral vision he spotted Sunnie greedily eying his bacon. That made his mission to get some food down her a lot easier. If he was going to use her services, she needed her strength every bit as much as he did. As tough as she was, she looked as though you could knock her over by whispering too loud.

"Do me a favor, will you?" he began. "I can't possibly eat all this food. But I also can't stand letting anything go to waste. My stomach is not steady enough yet to overload it. How about if you help me out?"

She shook her head.

"Just a piece of bacon or a slice of toast? It would sure save me from being queasy."

He decided not to push while he continued eating and thought out loud. "If the Navajo I was following was one of this so-called Skinwalker cult, and if the men you claim were following me out of Shiprock in that SUV were also Skinwalkers, then I keep coming back to...why? Why me?"

Without a word, she reached over and daintily picked up a piece of the bacon. He went back to his eggs.

"I've given it some thought," he continued after he swallowed. "The only thing I can come up with is maybe the murder I'm investigating has something to do with the Skinwalkers. It took place fifteen years ago. Was this new cult you mentioned operating that far back?"

Sunnie nibbled thoughtfully on the point of a half a

piece of toast. "Yeah, we'd already started hearing of the new Navajo Wolf about that time. But the real threat didn't become clear until around ten years ago."

"Hmm." He put down his fork and took a swig of coffee. "What if it's connected somehow? My investigation might uncover something the Skinwalkers don't want known. That could be one answer to why they're following me."

When he looked up, she popped into her mouth the last piece of an order of bacon he'd never even tasted. "Maybe."

"Listen," he said with as much sincerity in his voice as he could manage. "You're looking for a Skinwalker and you apparently know a lot about them. What if we work together on my investigation? I get the sense that they'll keep showing up wherever I go. I need your expertise to keep me out of trouble, and at the same time you can watch out for this man you're tracking. What do you say?"

"I say that's a very dangerous course to follow. You don't know *how* dangerous."

"But you're willing to give it a try?"

"I'll think about it." She eyed his unfinished eggs. "Hey, are you done with those?"

Chapter 6

The Navajo Wolf's mind cleared for the moment, but blurry visions and snippets of conversations still swam through his head. Had he made a mistake?

He'd just been informed the parchments were at last in Skinwalker possession. Everything should run smoothly from here on out. Yet something felt off, some component overlooked.

His men had already begun work on the parchment translations. Things were going as fast on that front as possible. But some thread left dangling continued to nag at the back of his conscious mind and begged for attention.

Breathing calmly, the Wolf tried to focus on the last couple of days. The Owl was certainly a traitor. That much he knew for sure. But the Wolf had determined to use every last drop of whatever intelligence remained in the traitor before his death. When it came down to it, the Wolf would let the Owl exchange the parchment translations for his own life. Neat. Simple.

But then, what else could be…?

His mind clicked over to consider the new beginning that was coming for the Skinwalker cult. When the parchments were at last translated and in his hands, his army would be unstoppable.

The idea of a new start brought him around to thoughts of the origin of his cult. It had been a long time since he'd remembered how clever he'd been in the beginning. Of how he'd made sure of every detail. Taken care to leave no loose ends.

The Owl had mentioned a stranger looking into an old murder. Could that have something to do with this odd certainty some problem had not been addressed? He felt assured nothing remained for anyone to find from that long-ago time. No clues. No traces.

But with a gasp and a frisson of shock, the old scene suddenly popped into Wolf's scattered mind. After a moment's reflection, he wondered if perhaps there really was one small detail he had not attended to. Still, that man had seemed so inconsequential at the time. His knowledge so slight.

On the eve of the dawning of the Skinwalkers' ultimate power, it would pay to be sure. The Wolf needed to resolve all potential problems, regardless of how remote, now, while there was time.

Time, he mused as the fog in his brain crept in again. The Wolf was about to wield the heavy sword of time as no one else had before him. He would be unstoppable.

In short order he would possess the ultimate Skinwalker destiny: immortality.

"I'll drive." Cisco held out his hand for the keys.

Sunnie pulled the sunglasses off her head and slipped them onto the bridge of her nose. The movement gave her a moment to appreciate the man standing before her.

Long and lean with strong shoulders and thick, muscular thighs, his body was hot and sweet. Mouthwatering. Just looking at him was setting off rockets in her toes.

"Forget it," she said in answer, as much to herself as to him.

"I'm a better driver than you are, sugar." He reached over and brushed a stray hair from her face. "And I'm not thrilled about ending upside down in some ditch. I'd rather take my chances with the bad guys, thanks."

Her first reaction to his touch was to rear back, but she stood in place and argued her point. "I know the best routes. I've spent most of my life on the reservation."

"We're off the rez in Farmington at the moment, don't forget." He dropped his hand and gave her a wry grin. "I spent hours in this town with a map the other day, scouting the streets looking for opportunities to find local gossips. I may know more about Farmington than even you do.

"You navigate and keep watch," he urged. "I'll do the driving."

When he was right, he was right. But she didn't have to like it. She dropped the keys into his hand, careful not to let their fingers touch in the process.

"We need to stop and get you a pair of sunglasses and a hat." She took off around the front of the Jeep and climbed into the passenger side.

Waiting until she'd buckled up, he started the engine. "My skin isn't exactly fair, as you may have noticed. Riding in an open car won't hurt me any."

"It will if the Skinwalkers or their friends catch sight of you. The hat and glasses are for covering up the bandage and your looks."

Shrugging a shoulder, he said, "I don't think that Navajo from the other night got a decent ID on me in the darkened bar. And I'm not sure those guys in the SUV last night caught sight of the bandage, either. I didn't catch any glimpses of them at all.

"Though," he continued with a note of reluctance in his voice, "I suppose a small disguise wouldn't actually be a terrible idea. I own sunglasses—they're in the duffel. And we can stop for a hat. But I'm betting the Jeep is a bigger giveaway than my looks."

Winds picked up strands of her hair and blew them crazily around her mouth. "Jeeps like this one are common on the rez," she told him as she shoved the wayward hair behind her ears. "Everybody uses them in desert country. If we're lucky, we won't be spotted."

He flashed her a grin. "And if we're not lucky?"

"We'll be dead."

"Dead?" The corners of his mouth curled in a wry smile. "Maybe they want *you* dead—or believe you're already dead—but I've gotten the feeling they want me alive for some reason."

"Then you'll just wish you were dead."

It wasn't so much that Cisco didn't believe her about the Jeep being a common sight. It was more that he took her word about not getting caught out in the open and being captured alive.

So when she'd given him the cross streets of a store where he could obtain a hat, he'd taken a roundabout route. Finding back alleys. Driving blocks out of the way and circling. He wound around until he found a parking spot within walking distance.

Grabbing his sunglasses from the side pocket of his duffel in the backseat, he turned to her. "You want to stay here?"

She shook her head and stepped out, slamming the Jeep's door behind her. "I know the high-pitched sound they make. I may even be able to recognize one of them in their human form. I should go."

He couldn't help the easy grin. "To protect me?"

With a quick frown, she took off down the street, staying in the shadows close to the buildings.

Glorious spirit, he mused. And fearless. The woman was a giant in a tiny, well-packed body.

There were few people on the streets for this time of the morning. A couple of SUVs drove past, but none of the traffic seemed threatening.

Right before coming to the corner, they had to step over the prone body of a drunk. Sunnie hid her face in her collar as the guy moaned and rolled over. But the old Navajo man never opened his eyes, and the two of them hurried past him in single file.

Was she so worried about supposed Skinwalkers in disguise that she wanted to hide from everyone on the streets?

"How come you're so skittish?" he asked in a hoarse whisper when he caught up.

"I told you—everyone thinks I'm dead. That's the way I want to keep it."

Had she told him that? He remembered her saying that the Skinwalkers didn't know she existed. But not *everyone* thought she was dead. He'd met a few people that clearly had seen her alive.

He didn't get a chance to ask anything else because they came to the storefront right then. He'd been ready for a Western-wear place, one where he would be able to buy a decent Stetson. Instead she headed into a sporting-goods store.

"Hold on," he said as he put a hand on her arm. "I was going for a Western hat, maybe a Stetson. Why here?"

"You want to blend in, not stand out, don't you?"

For this sort of work, blending in was good. "Yeah."

Sunnie moved down an aisle to a rack holding various team baseball caps. "Then pick your favorite team and try one on."

"A ball cap? Just a logo away from a gimme cap? No way."

She quirked one side of her mouth and rolled her eyes. "Even deadly Latino hombres can wear caps. Especially when every other man on the rez wears them, too."

"I could swear I've seen magazine photos showing men in Navajoland wearing Western hats."

Sunnie nodded as she pulled a couple of caps off the rack and handed him one. "Those who ride horses, either working horses or for the rodeos, wear them. I don't think my Jeep qualifies, do you?" She raised her eyebrows as she glanced up at him. "Weren't you paying attention to the other customers back at the restaurant?"

He guessed not. Which was really weird. Usually Cisco was well tuned-in to his surroundings. Like being able to recite accurate descriptions of people, he prided himself in always watching his back and keeping an eye on what was going on around him.

So where had his mind been this morning? One glance at Sunnie as she turned her back to try on a couple of caps herself made things perfectly clear. The shiny black hair pulled back in a soft ponytail drew his attention first. Then his gaze wandered down her straight back and the feminine curve of her waist, landing on her rounded bottom in the worn pair of jeans.

The tantalizing sight made him remember the lacy thongs he'd found in her backpack. Did she have a pair like those on under the jeans? In colors of pink, blue and sunshine-yellow, they had seemed so incongruous for the melancholy, practical woman sniper.

Once again he thought of how she might have a split personality. He'd seen no real evidence save for the Skinwalker story, but he grew more curious about her story every minute.

Fifteen minutes later, the two of them were back in the Jeep with University of New Mexico caps pulled down on their foreheads and sunglasses covering their eyes. As she gave him directions for driving south and leaving town the back way, he tried to distance himself from any further thoughts of her underwear. From any thoughts of her—period.

He was losing his edge. And he didn't want to die—or see her die—because of it.

She gave directions as Cisco drove them south on Highway 371. They kept going, passing by the stark landscapes of the Bisti Wilderness area and driving through the small town of Crownpoint.

As they moved farther away from the Four Corners area, Sunnie was careful to keep them just outside the Navajo border. The midday sky turned winter-gray and colored the vast emptiness of the western New Mexico landscape with a bleak look, the same as her current mood. Sandstone, shale, goat weed and chamisa…the whole of their world seemed pale and wan.

Turning west after Crownpoint, she found a way for them to skirt the city of Gallup. Taking Route 264 through the wide spots called Yah-Ta-Hey and Black Hat, they finally came back onto the reservation right at the Navajo Nation's capital of Window Rock—her temporary home.

Window Rock was not as far away from the Four Corners area as you could possibly go on the reservation. Not the way Page or Tuba City would be. But it was a good-size town with apartments and jobs and had seemed far enough removed from the bulk of the Skin-walker activity to keep her whereabouts unknown.

Still, you never knew what neighbor or coworker might be one of the evil ones. So she kept Cisco driving on busy streets until they turned down the narrow road toward her duplex apartment. She directed him to park the Jeep in back. And when he stopped, she grabbed his duffel and her pack, jumped out and raced to the kitchen door.

"Hold it," he said as he pocketed the Jeep's keys and caught up to her. "I can carry my own weight. You—"

"Quiet. We'll discuss everything inside." She fumbled her key in the lock but had the door open and then slammed shut behind them before he could even take another breath.

"I thought we would be safe here," he said as he glanced around her tiny one-bedroom apartment.

"I think we will be," she hedged, out of breath and out of excuses.

"Think? Yeah, thinking is so much better than knowing for sure." He winked at her and shook his head.

Ignoring him, she dumped the bags, went to the small stove and set a kettle of water on a burner to boil. "No one pays any attention to me. They're used to seeing the lonely waitress who lives here coming and going. But you're another story. I don't have men in my apartment."

"No? Not ever?"

"Not ever."

Taking off her coat, she waited for his, then hung them and both the hats on the rack behind the front door. "I hope you like tea. Or instant coffee. That's all I have. I don't have much food in the fridge, either."

She hadn't really expected to come back here after…after killing the Navajo Wolf. There had been little chance of her living long enough to go anywhere past the assassination.

But things had changed. The way to reach the Wolf was no longer as clear as it had once been. She figured his old route would be useless now and didn't know where to find him for sure. And even if she knew, she no longer had her rifle.

Sunnie found herself caught in a place she'd never thought she would be in again. Having to rely on someone else's help stung her pride. And that the someone was a man who challenged her both mentally and physically was a particular blow. He'd twisted her senses into knots and had destroyed her careful reserve with one touch of his lips.

"Tea will be fine," Cisco said evenly. "We can go out for food later, once we've checked around and made sure it'll be safe."

The kettle whistled and she made them both tea. While she did that, Cisco wandered over to her computer and flipped it on.

"Tell me this isn't dial-up," he moaned.

"It is. I'm not real sure broadband has arrived in Window Rock yet. Even if it has, I couldn't afford the service. I have a friend with fast access, but Reagan Long lives an hour and a half away. Do you want me to call her?"

"Reagan Long? Is she married to that tribal cop?"

Sunnie remembered how oddly Cisco had reacted to Hunter. Now he'd acted strangely to just the name Long.

"Reagan is Hunter's sister-in-law," she replied. "Married to his brother Kody. Hunter's wife is named

Bailey. She's a nice woman who tends her sick grand-mother most of the time."

"And is Kody Long also a cop?"

"Sort of," she answered, more hesitantly this time. What was the deal here? Why should he be so curious about the Long brothers? "Kody is an FBI agent. But he's also one of the Brotherhood. He's a good man you can count on.

"I'm sure Reagan and Kody wouldn't mind if we went to the house tonight so you could use their Internet access," she added carefully. "Should I call?"

"That's okay," he said, turning his back and going to work on her computer. "This may be slow, but I can still find the information I need eventually."

"Sugar?"

"Huh?" He turned a blank stare in her direction.

"Do you take sugar in your tea?"

He chuckled and gave her a warm, sensual look. "No sugar for me today, *míja*. I'll just suffer along with black while I try to make headway on recreating my research or gaining access to my notes stored online. Thanks, though."

Sunnie understood the double meaning he'd used for the word *sugar*. And the images his sexy tone of voice had put into her mind were stirring up a whirlwind of trouble in her body. Damned man.

She quietly set down the old mug with his tea right next to the computer and took herself off to face a nice cold shower.

A little later, clean and back in control, Sunnie dried off, changed into jeans and a gray sweatshirt and then put clean sheets on her bed. Cisco could sleep in the one bedroom, though his feet would probably dangle off the end of her single bed. She wouldn't have any trouble sleeping on the futon currently in the room passing as living and dining room, kitchen and office.

Walking back into that room, she came up behind him as he worked on the computer. "Are you getting anywhere?"

He kept on working. "I need more time."

She left him grumbling and went to pick up a few things from the grocery store. By the time she'd dragged the first of the many grocery sacks into the apartment, the sun had dropped below the western cliffs surrounding Window Rock. The light had disappeared this day with a cold, dull thud, not with the usual spectacular and colorful explosion of sunsets in Dinetah.

"Stop and eat something," she insisted when she put plates of hot mutton stew and corn tortillas on the card table that doubled as desk and dining table. "And talk to me about your research."

Turning his chair around, he pulled it closer to the table and the food. "This smells good. Did you make it?"

Laughing, she went to the fridge for a soda. "Do I seem like I'd be a good cook? It's takeout. They don't sell beer in Dinetah. You want a soda?"

He nodded, and she handed him one before sitting down in the only other chair in the entire apartment.

After letting him enjoy a few bites, her curiosity won out. "So...have you been getting anywhere online?"

"Some," he said as he took a swig from the can.

"How can I help? Tell me what you know about this old murder you're looking into."

Studying her with a wary stare, he pushed his plate back. "Fifteen years ago a man was shot on the rez. His body was found burned beyond recognition in the shell of his car. It appeared the car had been driven off a thousand-foot cliff and exploded at the bottom. At first, the investigators thought it was an accident. Until the autopsy found the bullet hole in his skull."

Sunnie thought of the newspaper clippings she'd seen in his duffel. "I would've been thirteen then. That was around the time my mother was diagnosed with cancer. As a typical teenage drama queen, I thought my life was over and wasn't paying much attention to anything else. The dead man's story does seem a little familiar, but I can't think of why. Did they find out who killed him?"

Cisco shook his head. "The victim was retired from the U.S. Marshal's service. He'd told his friends that one of the criminals he'd brought in years before had escaped from prison and that he'd been concerned the man would come after him for revenge. But when the FBI checked into it, they couldn't find any record of a prison break."

"So no one was ever charged?"

He shook his head again. "They identified the body with dental records and a wedding ring, but there wasn't much else left. No obvious clues and no witnesses."

"Are you saying you think the victim might not have been that same man? Couldn't they use DNA testing to be sure?"

"DNA wasn't as easy to identify back then, and at the time there didn't seem any doubt about who the dead man was." He straightened and picked up his soda. "I suppose

I believe the body was identified correctly. But I just don't understand why the case was never solved. That man had enemies. Why didn't they pin it on one of them?"

"Where was the car found?" It was the only question Sunnie could think to ask.

"In Canyon de Chelly, under a place on the rim called the Spider Rock Overlook."

"What? Have you ever been to the rim of Canyon de Chelly? You have to walk two hundred feet down a narrow path to the Spider Rock Overlook. It's amazing anyone could even get a car down that way."

Cisco looked thoughtful for a minute. "Can you take me there in the morning? I'd like to see it for myself."

She stood and began clearing the table. "Sure." Turning to the sink with their dirty dishes, she continued, "Are you going back online now?"

"Yeah. I'm trying to find a loose end. Some string everyone else missed."

"Anything I can do?"

He was quiet for so long she had to turn back to check on him.

"No," he finally said with a rough voice. "Just go on to bed. We need to get an early start. I want to be there before the tourists."

"Not many tourists this time of year. But we can start right after dawn. I'll stay up but keep out of your way. You might need to ask me a question." She couldn't quite look him in the eye. "Besides, you're taking the bed tonight. I'll be just fine on the futon over there."

She looked up in time to catch an odd expression on his face before he caught himself and turned to the computer screen. But she wasn't ready to question him about anything as personal as sleeping arrangements, so she dragged out of the closet the blanket her grandmother had woven as a girl and settled in on the futon to wait.

The next thing she knew, the gray light from a new day was peeking in through the miniblinds. Sunnie sat up, cleared her head and looked around the room. Cisco wasn't still sitting at the computer, where she'd last seen him. The clock on the wall said 5:00 a.m.

After a moment, she heard the shower running in the bathroom. The idea of Cisco naked in her shower gave her the shivers. A part of her longed to slip in beside him and take whatever comfort from body-to-body contact he would be willing to give.

But she wouldn't ask for casual sex from a man she didn't know.

For the first time she began to seriously wonder about the private life of Mr. Cisco Santiago. He'd had no trouble questioning her about her love life the night before. She hadn't told him everything, of course—wasn't even sure she could speak on that subject to anyone yet.

But he hadn't given her much information about himself in return, either. Now she was more than just curious concerning his business here on the reservation. She wanted to know the person underneath the dark hombre facade.

Suddenly grinning like an idiot, she promised herself that by tonight she would know more about him. Enough, at least, to feel comfortable going after whatever she wanted.

Chapter 7

Dawn played tag with the mountaintops, sneaking out here and there but never staying long enough to throw decent light on the road ahead. Cisco figured it was a good thing he was doing the driving this morning.

Sunnie had directed him to take them north into the mountains out of Window Rock. She'd claimed it was the back way to Canyon de Chelly and would give them less of a chance of being spotted. But it was one hell of a graded dirt road that curved and climbed through tough terrain, requiring him to constantly use the four-wheel drive.

Shooting a glance at Sunnie, who'd buckled in tight and held on to the door frame with all her might, Cisco couldn't help but think of last night and all the things she hadn't said. It had taken every bit of his willpower to let her sleep on the futon while he'd fought the computer, looking for answers or at least for more questions. And when he'd finally given up and headed for bed at 3:00 a.m., the frantic tossing and turning he'd done in the uncomfortably small single made the short night seem to go on forever.

He would've rather carried her into that tiny bed with him. Despite the close quarters—or because of them— the two could've held each other close and done fine. Most of his tossing had been due to thoughts of her in the other room all alone.

This morning, even after a cold shower and a hot cup of reheated coffee, he still didn't have his head together. But driving came second nature to him. No problem.

"Watch out for the skunk," Sunnie yelped.

Instead of downshifting to take the peak of the next hill, he suddenly had to jam on the brakes to miss a spotted skunk and felt the tires sinking backward on the grade. So far a jackrabbit, a raccoon and a mule deer had brought their progress to a halt. He had visions of what could have happened to them if Sunnie had been driving.

"How much farther?" he shouted without turning around. He wrestled the Jeep back under control and topped the hill.

"Not much. The turnoff for Three Turkey Ruins is coming up. We're almost there."

Glancing once again at the sleek beauty beside him, he wished for quiet time to have a conversation with her. There were things he wanted to know, now more than ever. Last night she'd casually slipped into the conversation that her mother had had cancer when she was a teen. Had the mother died? What about the rest of Sunnie's family?

She'd been deliberately silent concerning her past and her family. But he'd also been careful not to ask too many probing questions. Mainly because he hadn't wanted to discuss his own background. Now he began to wonder if her past might have some bearing on his investigation.

Just ahead he saw a small sign designating a loose gravel road as the way to Three Turkey Ruins. Beyond that, he drove the Jeep up another little grade and found himself back on a blacktop road.

"Take the immediate right turn there," she said, pointing northeast. "That's the way to Spider Rock Overlook. It's the last public access on the south rim."

The moment he swung the Jeep around and continued driving through seemingly flat but remote landscape, Cisco felt a change in the atmosphere. A sudden chill, regardless of the morning sun. An odd silence punctuated by shrieks from raptors circling high above them. Narrowing his lips and biting down on the urge to turn around, he pressed his foot to the accelerator and kept going.

In another twenty minutes he pulled into the small parking lot for the Spider Rock Overlook. "Pretty isolated out here," he muttered as he parked the car and climbed out.

"We like our sacred places isolated," Sunnie said with a nod. "Come on, there's the path to the viewing point."

It was a moderate descent on a narrow rock walk to the edge of the canyon. Cisco took his time following her and proceeded with caution. He wondered how a car could've accidentally run out of control this far off the road. The place was still too damned quiet, the air filled with something resembling static electricity.

At the rim, Sunnie stood with hands on hips, staring out at the thousand-foot drop and the spectacular sights beyond. A giant pinnacle, along with a smaller sister, rose straight up from the canyon floor to heights nearing the rim. The sandstone wonders looked close enough to reach out and touch. But of course the largest was probably a good mile away.

"Tsi na ash jeii," she whispered reverently.

Cisco was amazed to see this wonder of nature, with layer upon layer of deeply colored sandstone and slate, spread out into wide vistas below him. Maroon streaks marred the distant walls of canyon rock, while the burnt-rust color of desert varnish added interest to buttes and pinnacles of volcanic extrusions.

More stunning than any of the guidebooks or Internet panoramas had promised, the view was awesome. He suddenly felt rather reverent about the place himself.

"Spider Rock," Sunnie explained without taking her gaze away from the sight. Cisco turned to look at her. "This is a most sacred spot for Dine. One of our deities, Spider Woman, is said to live at the top of Spider Rock. It's our tradition that in the beginning, she taught Dine women how to weave. We owe her thanks for our warmth and also for much of our livelihoods.

"As children," Sunnie continued with a smile, "we're also told how Face Rock tells Spider Woman about naughty children and then carries them to the top of her rock, never to be seen again. The threat always kept me in line."

Cisco chuckled and moved closer to the edge. With no railing or other protection, he got a little too close. Pebbles slipped from under his feet, trickling down the sheer cliff walls and disappearing into the nothingness below. Another chill raced down his back, making him look around to see if anyone was watching their movements.

He stared down at the distant canyon floor, dotted with juniper, cottonwood and cactus. "Is there a trail that leads to the bottom? Or any way for me to scout around the spot where the car landed and burned?"

She shook her head and turned at last to face him. "No one is ever allowed into the canyon without a park ranger or a registered Navajo guide. Unless you live there."

"Live there? Where?"

"Farther upriver there are a few small Navajo ranches and farms. Not many anymore, because it's a hard life. The Navajo Nation will not allow electricity, running water or modern conveniences to be brought in to our sacred land. These days, most of the ranchers move out of the canyon to nearby houses with electricity and heat during winter."

"The murder took place in January," he said, thinking aloud. "So I'd guess there wouldn't have been many people around. No nosy neighbors and not many tourists."

"Just like now," Sunnie added as a stiff winter wind wrapped around their ankles and drove frigid air inside their clothes.

He needed to think over what he'd learned. More positive than ever there had been an odd tidbit in the notes or the news articles he'd seen last night, Cisco was sure some link to the canyon and the murder was hiding in plain sight. He'd looked right over it. But now that he understood more about the canyon, it was important to bring that hidden fact to light.

If he thought hard enough or gave himself enough time and space for consideration, he knew the knowledge would come to him.

"Is there anyplace around here where we can get a cup of coffee?"

"The Thunderbird Lodge has a restaurant," she said. "It's kind of rustic, but the food's good. Only a few minutes away."

He took her elbow and retraced their steps to the Jeep. Perhaps if he spent a while getting to know Sunnie better, his subconscious would work on the mysterious missing-link problem in the meantime.

Blowing on the steaming coffee, Cisco settled into the cracked vinyl booth and studied Sunnie over the rim of his mug. His nerves were raw, on edge, and every little detail about her seemed more vivid and earthy than ever.

She leaned her elbows on the scarred wood tabletop. "I can tell you a few other things about the canyon. Though I don't know as much as a guide would."

Her voice was low, sensual. It spilled like spun honey over his ears, igniting a fire in his groin that he needed to find a way to extinguish.

Anger, however irrational, was safer. Or was it? Now that he thought of it, he remembered noticing only a thin line between anger, fear and…hot lust.

Right this minute he needed neither anger nor lust. He needed sanity. "I'd really like you to tell me about your family. I think it's important for me to get to know you if we're going to work together."

She blinked, then forced aside a stray strand of her hair in a hasty movement. The idea of talking about herself must make her as nervous as it did him.

"There's nothing to tell. My family is either gone or might as well be." She hesitated only a moment before adding, "I'd much rather hear about your family."

"Oh, no, you don't," he said with a grin. "No turning the conversation to me until you've finished your story." He was determined not to let her slink away this time. "You said something last night about your mother getting cancer when you were thirteen. I take it she didn't live. That's too bad. Can you tell me about it?"

She narrowed her eyes at him but shrugged a shoulder as if it wouldn't hurt to talk. "She was sick for five years before she died. As the only girl in the family, it was my job to care for her. Watching her deteriorate was the hardest part."

"You were her caretaker? Throughout high school?"

"I didn't go to high school. There was no way. But I had a teacher who brought the work to my house. With her help, I managed to graduate on time. Uh…almost on time—just days after my mother passed away."

"That's tough. It must've changed you."

Sunnie nodded thoughtfully. "My father helped me through it and taught me many lessons. One of those was how women must sit with sorrow. But I didn't…"

She'd seemed ready to say something else but went

in another direction. "My mother's death did change me some. I felt I'd found my calling and decided to become a nurse. My father helped pay my way through college."

He'd known she was a nurse. It had been obvious from the beginning. He wondered why she wasn't still working as a nurse now, though he wasn't ready to push her yet.

"So where are your father and brothers?" he asked.

"My brothers left the reservation years ago. One joined the Army. Another went off to follow the rodeo. My baby brother got fed up with trying to find a job and just walked away. We've lost touch."

"And your father?"

Opening her mouth, she shook her head and looked down into her coffee mug. "He's gone now, too," she said in a rough whisper.

Well, obviously that was the part of her story where the pain lingered. He didn't like the remorse and guilt he'd clearly heard in her voice. Something about her father's death must have been life-altering and too difficult for her to discuss.

Interesting that his own father's death had also been a life-changing event for him. Feeling sympathetic but still not ready to give up everything about himself, he decided to tell her at least something in return for giving him a glimpse into her background.

"My high school years weren't anything to rave about. Don't think you missed out on much by skipping yours."

She glanced up, but the melancholy expression hadn't changed.

"My mother and I were living in Albuquerque," he added. "Mama had come across the border before I was born, leaving all her family behind. Just as I entered high school our circumstances…suddenly changed. We had to scratch and claw to find ways to survive. I allied myself with a gang, doing whatever was necessary to make money and stay alive."

"Is that where you got the scar?"

"Scars. Yes. I did a few things I wish I hadn't. But I survived. Got tough and got out. My mother wasn't so lucky. She died of a drug overdose a few years later."

He took a slug of strong, cold coffee that was thick enough to lube a car. He'd never before given anyone even a minor look into his background. Letting go of a tiny sliver of information about his family felt good. Relieving.

"I—I'm sorry you had to lose her that way," Sunnie said softly, searching his face for emotion.

"Don't be," he shot back, cutting her off and masking whatever feelings were left. "Things in the past should be over." But he knew both of them had one or two things in their pasts that still bothered them. And, oddly, each of their dark secrets seemed to center around their fathers.

"A big part of the Navajo philosophy tells us one should learn to recognize what's beyond one's human power to change." She shoved her coffee mug aside and reached out a hand to him. "It's the attitude that must be adjusted. People should strive to become content with the inevitable."

From across the table he took her hand. "And you live by that philosophy?"

"Hell, no," she said with a wry laugh. "But I wish I could."

Cisco relaxed and laughed, too. It was then that the

piece of information he'd been trying to remember came back to him in a flash.

He pulled his hand from hers, felt the loss but ignored it. "I've just thought of something. According to the news accounts, a Navajo guide was first to find the car wreck and the body at the bottom of the canyon. You think a guide might've been unusual in the canyon for that time of year? His name was, um, Shorty Tom, I think."

She tilted her head. "A guide might be there at any time of the year. Did he have tourists with him?"

"I don't know. The article didn't mention any. Do you think the man would still be around, maybe still guiding, after all these years?"

"Who knows? It's possible, I suppose." Sunni glanced around the restaurant. "Let's go. See the old woman at the cash register? She's known for her knowledge of Canyon de Chelly. Been living near here most of her life. I bet she knows the guides, both current and past. We can ask her."

They scooted out from the table and Cisco grabbed the check. He started for the register in the front, but Sunnie touched his arm and hung back.

"You do the asking," she whispered as she pulled the brim of her cap farther down on her forehead. "I don't know how good her eyesight is anymore, but I'd rather she didn't recognize me."

"Do you know her well?"

"Not really. But they carried my picture in all the papers around here when I—" She stopped herself and pursed her lips. "About six months ago. If I'm the one putting my face right up in hers, she might be more inclined to study it than most people are. I try hard not to make waves, so people barely look at me. And not everyone reads the paper in Dinetah, anyway."

She took a breath and continued. "But I bet she does. I'd rather she didn't even think I look familiar."

Cisco nodded, but he now had one more burning question he needed to ask. It would wait for a quiet moment.

There weren't any other customers in the place, so he strolled to the counter, flapped down the check and a ten-dollar bill. The ancient woman, with wrinkles the size of slot canyons covering her face, raised her chin and glanced at both him and Sunnie. But neither one of them seemed to interest her very much.

As she made change, Cisco said, "I'm looking for a canyon guide from about fifteen years ago. Maybe you could help me find him?"

"Looking for?" the old woman asked without glancing up.

"Let me rephrase that." Cisco did this sort of thing as a skip tracer and wondered how much it would end up costing him. "Would twenty bucks help me locate a guide I simply wish to talk to about something that happened fifteen years ago?"

"If you're not a cop, perhaps," she said quietly in a cigarette-roughened voice. Lifting her chin and narrowing her eyes, the old woman continued. "Try a name and see."

He pulled the twenty from his pocket and held it just out of her reach. "Not a cop. And we want to talk to a man named Shorty Tom."

"The man you seek no longer guides." She tugged the

twenty from his fingers and it disappeared under the counter. "But the son does. Joe Tom. Pick up his brochure from the rack over there on your way out."

Cisco was about to say something more when he felt Sunnie poking him in the back. "Thanks," he finished as the old woman handed him change from the ten.

The change was minus two bucks, but he decided it wasn't worth making a fuss over. They'd learned enough from the old lady to point them in the right direction and hopefully not expose Sunnie in the process.

With the brochure in hand, Cisco and Sunnie stepped from the front door. Immediately he knew another shift in atmosphere had taken over the parking lot. The air surrounding them crackled with mysterious impressions. Nothing looked wrong or smelled wrong. But whatever was different had not changed for the good.

Sunnie apparently felt it, too. She stiffened beside him and nearly ran full-out to the Jeep.

"Drive," she said before he'd even buckled in. "Turn back toward the south rim. This brochure says Joe Tom guides on horseback from the Totsonii Ranch. Most of the guides live right at the ranch and tend the horses when not guiding. Maybe he'll be there on a quiet day like today."

"You feel it, too, don't you?" He started the engine and blasted out of the lot.

She nodded. "I'm not sure what's happening. There's no buzz, but it sure feels like Skinwalker trouble."

He slowed the Jeep to the shoulder of the deserted blacktop. "Do you want to turn around? Go somewhere else?"

"No chance. Is anyone following us?"

"I'm too good for that." Shifting gears, Cisco drove back onto the road.

Rolling her eyes, she grimaced. "Too bad. I keep hoping we'll lure a Skinwalker out in the open."

He slammed on the brakes, throwing her forward and forcing her to brace herself against the dash. "What? I thought you didn't want to be recognized. You're *trying* to get one of them to come for you?"

"Not for *me, Naakaii*." He caught the glimmer of humor in her eyes, but she turned her face away and silently stared out at the landscape.

Cisco ground his teeth. So much for becoming friendly partners. Had she meant that? In his years of observing people as they made statements he'd found there was usually at least a kernel of truth in every joke. Was his presence worth no more to her than bait?

Why the hell was he still tangled up with this woman?

Putting his foot on the gas, he continued driving toward the ranch. He could take care of himself with the Skinwalkers. But he was through making her life easy. He'd demand all the information he needed from her— anytime he wanted. He'd be free to take other things, too. More intimate and physical things.

This time he wouldn't allow either of them to stop.

Sunnie left her hat pulled low and her sunglasses in place and spoke to Joe Tom in Navajo. Cisco remained cold and distant, still ticked over her little joke. Too bad she had only been half-serious. It would make her mission much easier if they could find a Skinwalker and follow him back to the Wolf.

That wasn't going to happen this minute, so she continued on with their plans. The guide, Joe Tom, told them his father Shorty was indeed still alive. Today the old man was working out in a far pasture on the ranch, with the brood mares.

Following the son's directions, they walked through a couple of empty corrals and traveled down gravel riding paths past several barns. When they came near the black railings of an isolated pasture, instead of finding the old man, they found nothing but horses.

"You think Shorty's gone somewhere?" Cisco asked quietly. "Like back to the ranch for dinner?"

She scanned the pasture, saw the mares tripping around. "I doubt it. Let's go see what's spooking the horses."

When she put her hand on the gate, Cisco laid his hand on hers. "Why don't you stay here? It might be a rattlesnake or something."

Jerking the gate open under his hand and giving him the most determined look she could manage, Sunnie said, "Yeah, or something. I'm going in. You stay here if you want."

He shook his head as she opened the gate and stepped inside. Following her in, he drew his gun and stayed low.

The glare from the sun, shining off rocks and grasses, prevented her from seeing the dead body in the far corner until she was nearly on top of it. Mares scattered away from the site. They ran from the two human strangers who'd invaded their territory. Ran from the mutilation and the horror that contaminated their domain.

"Hold it," Cisco said as he came up beside her. "I'll take it from here. Go on back and call the police."

But it was already too late. Too late to keep her from seeing. Too late to save poor old Shorty Tom.

Chapter 8

"This must've been done by an animal," Cisco murmured aloud as he holstered his weapon and knelt to examine the body.

Looking for answers while not touching or ruining the evidence, he noted no bullet wounds could be seen in the mass of bloody pulp that had once been Shorty Tom. But it also seemed unlikely the man's death had been caused by fists or any blunt weapons. Both skin and clothing lay shredded in the dust and looked as though they been torn by sharp claws.

The body had been lying there for a while. Shiny black beetles had already arrived to feed on the decay.

"Not an ordinary animal." Sunnie spoke without a single crack in her voice. "Ordinary animals strike from either fear or hunger. The monster who did this felt neither."

He glanced up. Her face was shaded by sunglasses and hat, and he couldn't judge her mood. But she seemed much steadier than he felt.

Not a stranger to death himself, he'd unfortunately witnessed his share of murders. Cisco had never seen anything like this killing before, though. Fighting a queasy stomach, he swallowed hard.

Glancing back at the body, he also swallowed a tiny taste of panic. "Skinwalkers?"

She gave him a sharp nod. "What I don't understand is why."

"You don't suppose they somehow found out I wanted to talk to him?" Cisco didn't like the sudden thought that he might be the real cause of this old man's death.

"Why would that make them want to kill him?" Sunnie pulled her cell phone from her pocket. "What does an old unsolved murder have to do with Skinwalkers?"

He shrugged. "No clue. But I also don't know why they're trying to find me. Are you going to call the Navajo police?"

"The Brotherhood," she said soberly. "We need help. Shorty's son might think we had something to do with this. We'll have to clear out of here without being seen by anyone else."

She placed her call and took instructions over the phone. When she was done, she hung up and turned to him.

"I hope you're up for a walk," she said with a thin smile. "There's an old Navajo trail behind the hill there that will take us beyond the backside of the ranch and then circle around to Three Turkey Ruins. The Brotherhood will take care of talking to the son and dealing with the body. Someone will meet us in my Jeep."

"Is it far to Three Turkey Ruins?"

"A couple of miles. But it's fairly rough desert."

She was so cool. *Steely* might even say it better. His stomach had finally settled, but he'd found a whole new respect for her. And for the destruction the Skinwalkers could wreak.

"I can make it if you can," he said with a steady tone in his voice.

"Don't worry about me." She turned her back to the body and began moving away but continued speaking over her shoulder. "Better keep your gun handy. There's a lot more to worry about from the Skinwalkers than from anything else in the desert."

"Do you think they're looking for us now?" He was already reaching for the .38 under his coat.

"I don't know why they would be. But with Skinwalkers, you can't count on anything."

Their walk through the rock, sand and sage seemed interminable. They'd agreed to remain quiet, trying not to draw attention to their movements. Cisco took the time to study Sunnie in the light of day.

She moved though the brush like an animal. With head held high but body bent in stealth, she stalked across the high plain using the graceful movements of a mountain lion—or a black panther.

He took note of the straight nose, the full and firm mouth. The eyes behind the shades so dark brown they were ebony. In the filtered sunlight, dappled occasionally between deep gray clouds, the tumble of her coal-colored hair hanging below the cap sparkled like black ice.

Cisco found himself in the midst of turbulent emotions where she was concerned. And he didn't like it one bit.

Her dainty limbs and the slender curves hidden by the tough outdoor clothing gave him lustful urges that drove fists of fog into his normally sharp mind. A crazy admiration for the tiny woman who possessed both strength and detachment stirred within his bones. Her words could be stinging, yet her eyes sometimes filled with such need and vulnerability that he felt bound to defend her with his life.

Something had to give between the two of them soon. He was on the verge of becoming useless as an investigator. And he couldn't let that happen. This was the most important investigation of his life.

Out in front, Sunnie was surprised to see they'd arrived early as she rounded one of the ten-foot-high boulders beside the path. The hogans and shacks of the village of Three Turkey Ruins were about four hundred feet straight ahead. She raised her hand to silently tell Cisco to halt behind her.

He came up beside her and stood, staring in quiet at the afternoon scene in the distance. When a man a couple hundred yards away left his mobile home and got into a pickup, Cisco made a move that took her by surprise. Backing her into a rock crevice, he crushed in close beside her.

"Hey, stop pushing me," she whispered with annoyance.

"Shush." He lifted a hand and stroked her hair. "Don't move. We wouldn't want to alert the Skinwalkers."

Undone by the warmth of his body pressing tightly against her own, Sunnie was amazed as wisps of a smoldering fire combusted low in her belly. What was it between them that could explode so erotically and so fast?

"You did a good job leading us here without being seen," he said softly. Lifting her chin, he let his eyes provide a mirror to what she was feeling. "Not many women could've faced that horror and then marched us two miles through the remote desert without a word of complaint."

"I'm not like most women."

"So I've noticed." He lowered his head so that his mouth was within a whisper's breath of her lips. "And I'm not like most men."

Knowing what his intentions were, she could've shoved him away. But this time she wanted the feel of his mouth on her own. Wanted to experience the flames there, as well as throughout the rest of her body, especially in every place touching his.

The actual coming together of their lips was no more than the lightest brush. So easygoing it seemed almost casual. The tender touch softened her muscles and made her growing need rise all the way to the tips of her breasts.

A bit weak in the knees, she clung to him. And tried to tell herself it meant nothing. *He* meant nothing but the potential for finding the Skinwalkers. But just maybe…he could also manage to soothe the growing fire he had already ignited within her in the meantime.

Being physically close to this man did not necessarily mean anything but simple pleasure.

Cisco murmured incoherently against her mouth, moved to kiss his way down her throat. "I want you, *mija*. And have since the beginning. I want you in my bed. Can't concentrate on much else anymore."

Sunnie thought of telling him she didn't even go to bed with friends, let alone with dangerous strangers who had mysterious intentions. But in truth she wanted him, too. Badly. Urgently.

Lifting his head, he gazed deeply into her eyes. "This isn't the place. Though our time is close. Count it in hours, not days." He backed off then, leaving her smoldering in the dusky shadows.

She let out a breath, tried to tamp down on the flames but felt them reignite in annoyance instead. "Don't be so smug and sure of yourself, Santiago. I say when things happen between us. Don't forget it."

Taking her hand, he grinned in the most irritating way. "Just keep thinking about us, then, sugar. And we'll see."

Damn the man. It was going to be next to impossible for her to think of much else now.

He wasn't happy to let go of her hand. But when Sunnie's Jeep and another vehicle approached their hiding spot and slowed, Cisco released her, squared his shoulders and walked behind Sunnie out into the open.

A tall, lean Navajo man with soft eyes climbed out of the Jeep and moved toward them. Once the other vehicle was close enough to get a good look, he saw it was one of the white SUVs used by the Navajo Nation Department of Public Safety. Hell, he had hoped to avoid meeting up with tribal cop Hunter Long again.

To his surprise, the other driver wasn't Hunter. As she stepped from the SUV and stood at attention beside the door, he was intrigued to see the driver was a Navajo woman officer dressed in uniform.

Sunnie introduced him to the man who'd driven her Jeep, and Cisco noticed the guy's brown eyes were penetrating and all-seeing. Something about the strange eyes said the man might know more than was knowable. But Cisco didn't feel threatened. In fact, if anything, he felt nothing but benign concern coming from the other man.

"Cisco meet Lucas Tso." Sunnie finished with the intros. "He's a member of the Brotherhood."

"I figured that," Cisco said as he acknowledged the other man with a nod. "Tell us what the Brotherhood has learned that can help us."

Lucas smiled at him. "A man who gets to the point. Okay. But first I'll quiet Sunnie's concerns by letting you know the body has been dealt with. Removed and on the way to burial."

Sunnie's concerns? Cisco hadn't imagined the tough but beautiful woman would have any great concerns that needed to be quieted.

"Sunnie tries to turn her back on her Navajo heritage," Lucas told him as though he'd heard Cisco's thoughts. "But it is our Way to handle death by prescribed methods. Her heritage is an integral part of her being, one she cannot ignore.

"The son of the one who died is grieving," Lucas went on. "But he knows by whose evil power the murder was committed and holds no animosity toward either of the people who found the body. He thought you were old customers of Shorty's. He does not know your names, nor has he asked."

Sunnie nodded. "That's good. For public knowledge, I would assume Kody Long has supposedly opened an FBI investigation into the murder, right?"

Kody Long. The other man Cisco had hoped he would be able to avoid.

Lucas shook his head. "Any news accounts will say the man who died was killed by a wild beast in defense of his mares."

"Very neat," Cisco muttered. "So why are the Navajo police still interested in us?" He tilted his head to indicate he was referring to the woman officer standing by the SUV.

"The officer is my wife, Teal. She only waits to drive me back to my truck."

"What have you found out about the Skinwalkers?" Cisco demanded in a change of subject. "Particularly the murderers. Are they still around? Out to find me?"

Lucas stood, watching him closely for a moment. To Cisco it almost felt as if he were under a microscope.

"We know a Skinwalker was responsible," Lucas finally said. "But we don't yet know the motive. I take it you think you do know the reason for this death?"

Cisco held his tongue. While the other man was studying him, he could've sworn Lucas was trying to see inside his mind. But Cisco had worked to block his own consciousness and turn his mind blank. He wasn't about to say or do anything to change that now.

Turning to Sunnie, Lucas said, "What did you want with the one who died? Why had you two come all this way to talk to an old man?"

Cisco wasn't sure what Sunnie could say. Whatever it was, he feared it would be too much. He didn't want the Brotherhood involved in his investigation in any way. For several reasons.

Sunnie lifted her chin, removed her sunglasses and stared Lucas in the eye. "It's up to Cisco to tell you his purpose. I am only his nurse."

Lucas grinned at her. "Yeah, that's likely." The Brotherhood member shook his head and seemed to give in.

Then Lucas shifted back to Cisco. "Your nurse is important to the Brotherhood. We would take it badly if anything happened to her while she's with you. Whatever it is you're seeking on the reservation, take care not to involve her.

"From everything we can find," Lucas added, "the Skinwalker who committed the crime has disappeared back into his wicked shadows. There seems to be no disturbance left in the surrounding area. You two should be free to leave or stay as you will."

Lucas turned, began walking away, then turned back. "Your wound has healed, Mr. Santiago. Return to Raven Wash Clinic and have Dr. Wauneka remove the sutures. We wouldn't want you dying of an avoidable infection before you can leave Navajoland." With that and a wry grin, the strange Brotherhood member swiveled and quickly moved to join his wife in her SUV.

Cisco touched the bandage on his forehead under the cap. He'd forgotten all about the wound and thought the dressing had been covered over by the shadow of the brim. How had Lucas Tso spotted it?

He looked over to Sunnie. "Is that guy for real?"

"Oh, yeah. Quite real. But you don't want to know all the things he can do."

No, Cisco thought not. Whatever Lucas could do would probably sound like a fairy tale—or a nightmare. And right now Cisco needed all his senses and a good dose of reality. A murder had been committed. A murder that might have been caused by an evil human who could change himself into the form of an animal with supernatural powers.

Add to *that* fantastic tale the ridiculous yet sublime pull Cisco felt coming from Sunnie, and he was already in fantasyland. She was a woman of secrets. But the strength inside her glowed right through her skin to drive him crazy. Even with irritation written on her face, she was as beautiful as a work of art and as sexy as hell.

He'd meant every word he'd said to her. Before this day was through, they would know each other much more intimately.

That was just about all the fantasy he could stand for the moment.

Sunnie sat in the passenger seat freezing her tail off. It was getting colder. She'd hoped, since the winds had temporarily died down, the afternoon temperatures would've warmed up some. But no such luck.

Wishing for a car with a top and a decent heater, she

wondered why she'd ever picked an old, open Jeep to drive. Oh, yeah, she remembered now. Money. She'd needed a four-wheel-drive vehicle that could take her everyplace in Dinetah she wanted to go. And she'd wanted something that wouldn't stand out and bring her unwanted attention. The Jeep was all she could afford at the time.

Cisco drove them up to a crossroads and stopped. "Where to? You want to go back to your place so I can do more work on the computer?"

She shook her head. "Not yet."

From the instant he'd pushed them into the crevice and given her that drugging kiss she'd known what their next stop alone would mean. The way her body had quivered in response to him was clear. Her aroused state had been so immediate and so fierce she'd had to push him away or succumb to the desire right there in the boulder's shadow. Annoyance had saved her that time, but she knew their moment was near.

"Let's go over the pass to Raven Wash Clinic. Get Ben to take out your sutures."

Cisco threw her an icy glance. "The damn wound is fine. If the sutures need to come out, I can do it myself. I wasn't too crazy about that veiled threat from Lucas Tso. I'm not leaving the reservation until I finish my investigation. None of the Brotherhood is exactly at the top of my good list at the moment."

"Oh, please, Mr. Macho. You need a doctor to judge how well the wound is healing. Lucas Tso is known to be right about things most of the time. If it's infected, you might need antibiotics. You can't very well continue your investigation if you're too sick with a fever or in the hospital on an IV drip."

Scowling, Cisco grudgingly agreed. She gave him driving directions, then folded her arms around her body for warmth and sat back.

It was a good thing Cisco hadn't wanted to hear about all the things Lucas could do. Some of them, like talking to the birds and receiving answers, were so beyond belief she barely accepted them herself. And she'd actually seen them.

Lucas Tso was a good man—she knew that, too. An artist and silversmith, he'd been known as a sensitive, one who could see others' thoughts. That is, he had been until his new wife, Teal, had shown up on the reservation. Things changed for him then. As they'd fallen in love, Lucas saw into people's minds less and less. Today he still could read people better than most, but the thoughts of others were now blocked to him.

He was still the only Brotherhood member who spoke the language of the Bird People. And the birds were great allies of the Navajo in their struggles against the Skinwalkers. His skill and his gentle kindness made Lucas one of her favorite people.

Another turn at the junction near the Lukachukai Chapter House brought them to the slow climb up and over the Chuska Mountains. Sunnie both loved and hated this route. It wasn't one she traveled often. The haunting beauty of the sheer drop-offs and gigantic boulders, along with the spicy scent of ponderosa and piñons, always made her melancholy as she wished for things that could not be.

Her father's mother had once lived in these mountains. Sunnie's happy memories of being a girl and traveling with her beloved father to visit her *anali* always ended, like every other thought of her father, in the violence and pain of watching him die.

Light snowflakes began to fall as the Jeep neared the peak of the pass. Staying warm became her newest obsession. She fiddled with the heater.

"Do you have some other vehicle to drive during the winter months?" Cisco asked.

Shaking her head, she decided to have a little fun and annoy him again. Purely out of a desperate need to alleviate the painful thoughts, of course.

"Wussing out on me, *Naakaii?* You wouldn't think a dash of cold weather could faze a man with so much heat and passion bottled up inside that he can't keep his hands to himself."

Grabbing the steering wheel in a white-knuckle grip, Cisco scowled over at her. The searing-hot gaze was back in his eyes, so intense and obviously sexual it caused her breath to hitch in her throat. She'd better learn to stop teasing the man.

"Tell me you don't like my hands on you," he began in a voice lowered to steely softness. "Tell me you don't want me as much as I want you, and then I'll start keeping my hands to myself."

His scowl turned to a seductive smile, so intimate and sensual she felt herself trembling inside. Why had she pushed him? What on earth had gotten into her?

As clumps of new wet snow began to stick to everything in sight, Sunnie vowed to put her mind back on the prize. The Navajo Wolf's death was her real goal. Giving in to desire with Cisco was nothing but a minor detour. Passion with him could only be an indulgence and would mean time away from the hunt she simply couldn't afford.

The incompetence of his men brought out fury in the Navajo Wolf. But anger would cause only further damage to his sick body. He had no time left to waste and no strength available to force his will.

"Why haven't you translated those parchments?" he demanded of the Owl. "If you're having so much trouble, just bring me that Brotherhood warrior Michael Ayze. He's always been the smartest one over there at the Dine College—unlike you, Owl."

The Wolf's words were designed to nip at the pride of the Dine college professor who turned himself into the Skinwalker Burrowing Owl. But maybe the man known to the Navajo world as Professor Richard Yellowhorse, assistant and friend to the brilliant Michael Ayze, needed a bigger shove in the right direction. If it was the last act of the dying Navajo Wolf, he would make this lazy bastard Owl do what he'd promised and obtain the translations.

The Burrowing Owl watched his superior closely, gritted his teeth and held his tongue. How he would love to shove a knife into the evil heart of the Wolf and be done with it. It would be a pleasure to see the end of the grand master of the Skinwalkers. But the time was not right. There were too many loose ends still flapping in the breeze and inviting trouble.

"The Brotherhood members have found ways to shield themselves from our magic," he finally said as an answer to the Wolf. "They are too powerful for us to capture."

"There should be a way to blackmail or bribe them, then," the Wolf argued. "I must have Ayze to make those translations. Find a weak link. How about Ayze's new bride? The one who speaks to ghosts. Capture her and Ayze will do as we wish."

The Owl shook his head. What an idiot the Wolf had become. "That woman is shielded by the ancestors. No evil can break through their spiritual power."

The Wolf waved away his objections. "One of the other women, then. There must be one that isn't always guarded and may be approached. One that all the Brotherhood would gladly die to save."

There was one woman, the Owl thought, who might be easier to capture. Now that she had come to mind, he was also sure her kidnapping would bring Michael Ayze and the others to heel. Not a half-bad idea even if it had been the Wolf's.

The Owl would put a plan in motion to reach the woman. And, meanwhile, he was still trying to get a handle on the dark stranger. Earlier he'd gotten the glimmer of an idea as to where he might be able to pick up the man's trail.

They knew the stranger had been injured in a shooting that first night. There had been blood in his car. And the Owl had a pretty good idea where a man who was not a Skinwalker might go to find help with his injury.

Chapter 9

Their road wound over the rocky mountaintop and
snaked down through pines on the western slope. The
snowfall was thick and numbing, but ice and sleet had
not formed at this altitude yet. The four-wheel drive still
gave the tires a good grip against the crunchy new
flakes. Cisco supposed things could be worse.

Then they were worse. Seeing ahead became prob-
lematic. The ancient windshield wipers could barely
keep up with the accumulation of fresh snow. Maybe as
they dropped in elevation the heavy precipitation would
level off to a manageable level. Much more of the stuff
at this rate, and they would have to shovel their way
down the mountain.

A blast of arctic wind sent stinging, frosty snow
sliding down the back of his neck. Uncomfortable and

getting wetter by the minute, Cisco checked on Sunnie in the seat beside him.

Her body shook uncontrollably as she tried to protect herself from the bitter and biting wind by pulling her coat collar up and scrunching down in the seat. He needed to get her out of this storm in a hurry.

"Is there someplace where we can find shelter and warm up?" he asked over the wind's roar.

"There used to be a trading post at Red Rock that served coffee," she mumbled in a barely audible voice as she shivered in the frigid air. "Another five miles ahead. But I'm not sure it's still there. It's been a long time since I've come this way."

Cisco hoped they could find that place or another soon, because he wasn't sure she would make it much farther. By the time he'd spotted the Red Rock road sign, the snow had actually quit falling but the winds had picked up even more. Drifts were blowing over the roads, and seeing was next to impossible. Sunnie's exposed skin was developing an unhealthy blue tinge.

He located the old trading post sign, but the place looked deserted. Next to it he noticed a gas station with lights still on in the gloom of the late-afternoon storm. That would have to do.

After he parked, they stepped out into half a foot of sloppy snow, and Sunnie yelled to him over the wind.

"There's a tarp and blanket. Let's cover the seats."

He would rather not have taken the time. But she insisted, reaching into a compartment and tugging a tarp free. Helping Sunnie cover the front seats with the heavy plastic tarp and watching her shiver, Cisco made a quick decision that the blanket would not be used as an additional Jeep top and was going inside with them.

In sixty seconds he had the heavy Navajo blanket in hand and hustled them both into the station.

The lone attendant took one look at Sunnie and not only offered them coffee but also volunteered to share his hot supper. Cisco found them a couple of stools at the single counter filled with newspapers. He shoved the papers out of the way and wrapped the blanket around Sunnie as she sat.

Within ten minutes the coffee had warmed them up enough so that Sunnie's shivering had stopped. The attendant was in a back room, nuking his posole supper and splitting it up three ways.

"I don't like the idea of eating that man's supper," Sunnie mumbled over the rim of her paper coffee cup. "If you're hungry, you should just stick to eating chips or crackers from the snack machines."

"Hunger isn't the point. You need sustenance and something hot to warm you from the inside out. Don't insult the man by turning down his offer and making yourself sick."

She frowned and finished her coffee. He could see the irritation written over her face once again. But, hell, was she trying to kill herself? She didn't have near enough fat on her body to stay out in the glacial air as long as she had. It seemed to Cisco a matter of life or death to raise her body temperature as quickly as possible.

After the attendant brought bowls of piping-hot stew and warm corn tortillas, he left them alone to eat. Cisco watched Sunnie choke down a couple of bites and then lower her plastic spoon. He offered her a tortilla and waited until she took a bite before he ate anything himself.

Perhaps he should try talking in order to take her mind off the food so she would absently eat more. The last time he'd tried such a thing, it had worked fairly well. Her talking—not his, of course. He thought of several questions she had never answered.

The one that came out of his mouth first surprised him. "You said once you'd been engaged but that it ended badly. Tell me what happened."

"What—now?" Her eyes shone with something that might have been amusement. Or maybe she was feverish.

He picked up her spoon, dipped it into the stew and held it out to her. "Why not? Take another bite and then talk to me while you continue eating."

Sunnie ate the spoonful as he'd asked but wondered if she was up to rehashing the old wounds. When she looked into Cisco's sympathetic eyes, though, she saw a gentleness, a warmth. It almost threw her off. She couldn't remember the last time she'd felt as though someone was trying to comfort her and cushion her pain.

She flashed back to the time when she'd first become engaged and thought her world was finally going in the right direction. Good-looking Louis Singleton, the athletic director at the local high school, had been quite a catch for a motherless young nurse with plain looks and little family around to guide her. But he had never looked at her with the same compassion as Cisco. In fact, Louis had seldom looked at her at all. Still, her father urged her to accept Louis's marriage proposal, and so she had.

Cisco touched her arm. "If this is too painful…"

She shook her head and slid her arm out from under his hand. His touch made her feel…a connection. But she didn't want to feel anything. Oh, she didn't mind experiencing the searing heat between them. That at least was something she could push aside when necessary. Real feelings made her weak. And she wouldn't allow them.

In lieu of dwelling on feelings—on him—she took another spoonful of stew and began to answer his question. "Louis—that was his name—was a respectable man. At first he was kind to me. I thought our life together was destined to be long and happy, full of family and contentment."

"Did you love each other?" Cisco interjected.

The question was not one she'd spent time on before. "To tell you the truth, I think he did love me, in his way."

But then again, at the end, Louis Singleton hadn't been aware of love or friendship or any other human emotion. His humanity had been lost.

"And you? How did you feel about him?"

"Um, well it wasn't the kind of romantic love you hear about all the time on T.V. But I was happy to be with him. He seemed to offer the long-term friendship and caring that I'd lost when my mother died and my brothers left home. He was a replacement family—and exactly what I thought I wanted at the time."

Taking a second to think what to say next, Sunnie ate another bite of stew and followed it with the rest of the corn tortilla. "Besides, he was full of exuberance and passion for new thoughts and ideas. That made him different than any other Navajo I had ever known. It made him fascinating."

"What kind of new ideas? What was he into?"

"Well, that's just it. I didn't know, didn't realize for months, that this exciting secret society he belonged to was the Skinwalker cult."

Cisco narrowed his gaze. "How could you not know?"

A new lump of anger threatened to well up in her throat. But she attempted to swallow it by finishing off the stew.

"It wasn't like any of them came right out and said, 'Hey, come on down and sign up to get your evil witchcraft with us.' I don't think even Louis understood what he was getting into until it was too late."

The memory of her guilt, of what she'd done in the name of finding happiness, made her stomach queasy, and she dropped her spoon. "Their philosophy sounded so modern and right. It was the only time I'd ever heard anyone say you wouldn't find true happiness until you loved yourself first. The idea still makes a kind of sense, even though now I see how anti-Navajo a sentiment like that is. It's the reverse of everything we're taught."

"How far into the witchcraft did you go?"

"Not far," she said and let the annoyance show in her voice. "Mostly I only did what Louis asked me to do. He used me…" She stopped herself, took a breath and went on. "I *let him* use me to obtain information from the Brotherhood. I spied for him and gave others false information, hoping to lead them in wild directions off his trail."

"What happened? How did you get away from him?"

Cisco's voice had become deep and rich with a hint of a Latin accent and more than a hint of caring.

Sunnie stared into his fathomless gray eyes, found emotion there she didn't recognize. The heat of it flowed over her skin and seeped into her spirit. This was an odd, new feeling. But one that gave her more strength.

"The Brotherhood found out about Louis when they were involved in a battle with the Skinwalkers. When Louis was killed, the Brotherhood came to me for answers about him—about me. But most of the men of the Brotherhood are distant cousins and they insisted on helping me find my lost spirit."

"How'd they do that?"

"They have special ceremonies and medicines they've designed using ancient texts. They know how to sing chants to form invisible shields around places so that the Skinwalkers can't get through. They had me go through retraining in Navajo traditions. It took weeks, but I was finally cured."

"Then what?"

The devilish memory came fast and furious, but she kept the unwanted thoughts from showing on her face. "The Brotherhood made up a whole new identity for me. So I could hide in plain sight."

"Why? Why hide at all?"

"I'd seen the Wolf in his human persona. I even went with Louis once to the Skinwalker mansion hideout."

"Whoa." Cisco reached out and took her hands in his. "That's scary."

"Yeah, it was. I guess finding me became the Wolf's top priority. He didn't want anyone not controlled by the

Skinwalker cult to have that much information about them. He sent people looking for me."

"Did he? Did they find your hiding spot? What happened?"

The worst thing imaginable was what happened. But she wasn't ready yet to say the words. Wasn't ready to give up that one last thread of her sanity.

So she told him what she could. "It took them about a year to find me, to come upon a foolproof way of bringing me out into the open."

With a sigh and a wish to change the past, Sunnie gave him the most basic information. "They hurt me when they caught up, thought they'd killed me. And I died."

Stunned, Cisco tried to get her to tell him how it had happened. How the hell the Skinwalkers had managed to find her. But whatever those memories were, they seemed too difficult for her to think about, let alone say aloud.

Taking a breath, he went to find the station attendant for more coffee and to pay whatever they owed. Coming back to her with two steaming cups, Cisco decided she needed to get at least the ending of that story out. Plus, he was curious about the practicalities.

He handed her one of the cups and sat down. "I'm guessing since you're sitting here alive and—" he hesitated, tried to find words that wouldn't push her away "—and in gorgeous form, you didn't really die but only appeared to. How'd you manage it?"

"The Brotherhood helped me." She blew on the coffee and waited for it to cool. "Dr. Ben and his wife healed my wounds in secret. And in the meantime the rest of the Brotherhood held a funeral service. They actually put a box into the ground supposedly holding my remains. As far as the rest of Dinetah knows, I'm dead and buried."

"So that's why you're going by a different name now. What was your name before?"

She only smiled at him in the sad and resolute way she had done several times before. "It doesn't matter. The person who carried the name is gone for good. What you see when you look at Sunnie Begay now is what matters."

He didn't believe that was strictly true. There had already been glimpses of the person she'd been before. So much so, at times he'd thought she must have a split personality.

"Will you ever go back to nursing?" he asked.

"I doubt I'll have the opportunity."

Well, that comment hadn't said much. It sounded as though she might want to go back but didn't think such a thing would be possible for some reason. Did she believe the Skinwalkers would win the war in the end?

He wouldn't push her for more answers. Not now. All he could think of at the moment was taking her home and keeping her out of sight.

"The storm's letting up," she said. "If we can get a few more miles down the road now, it'll be easier to reach Raven Wash Clinic. It seldom snows much on the plain. And even when it does, it's never as deep as it gets up here in the mountains."

"I don't think it's strictly necessary for us to continue the plan of going to the clinic," he muttered. "Let's just go back to your place."

She shook her head. "We can't go back by the mountain roads. Not with this storm. The only other way to reach my apartment takes us right past the clinic."

"You mean we'll have to go the long way around to Window Rock, like we did the last time?" He couldn't imagine her surviving the trip in this frigid weather.

"Maybe we'll come up with another idea," she said weakly. "But first you get your sutures removed."

This time it was Cisco who absently shook his head. But as he helped her off the stool and tightened the blanket around her body, he reminded himself to have patience. She'd been lied to, had her whole life turned upside down and finally had been attacked and buried in a phantom ceremony. It seemed clear she'd made herself much tougher in order to stand up to the strain.

But he had a good idea that deep inside she wasn't as strong as she pretended to be. And he vowed to get to the bottom of this special woman's secrets.

The rest of the trip down the mountainside was uneventful, but the winds still blew bitterly cold. Cisco couldn't have been happier to see the sign for Raven Wash Clinic. He pulled into the lot and escorted Sunnie inside.

Warm and almost cozy inside the sterile rooms of the clinic, the place suddenly seemed welcoming—rather more like home than he remembered from the last time they'd been here. He let a nurse settle them into an examining room while she chattered away to Sunnie.

Instead of the stench of medicine and sickness, this afternoon the smells of sage and herbs and of food cooking somewhere unseen pleasantly took their places.

He breathed in deep and got a light whiff of the aroma of cinnamon. Odd for a western medical clinic. But perhaps not so odd for a Navajo medicine man's clinic.

It occurred to him then: the smell was very like the special scent that sometimes surrounded Sunnie. He'd never been able to place it before.

Cinnamon. Not a usual southwestern United States spice. But the slightly sweet, mostly tart scent fit her perfectly.

The nurse left and returned in a few minutes with herb tea for both of them. "Dr. Wauneka says the tea will warm you. Drink it—his orders. He'll be with you in a few minutes."

Cisco sat on the exam table and watched Sunnie sipping her tea. Her skin had already begun returning to its natural silken bronze color. Her eyes had finally lost that glazed look.

He came to an immediate decision. They would not be spending much more time in her open-topped Jeep. It was too dangerous in this weather, no matter that she'd said it was a popular vehicle on the rez and good for a disguise.

"Ya'at'eeh." Ben Wauneka opened the door and spoke as he entered. "What can I do for you two in such a storm?"

Sunnie set down her mug. "Cisco's here to have his sutures removed and the wound checked."

The doctor raised an eyebrow at her remark. "I'll bet you've removed at least a thousand sutures in your career. Why come all the way here? Why not just do it yourself?"

"I tried to tell her…."

"Lucas Tso said the wound might be infected," she interrupted. "We came to have you check it over."

Ben stepped to Cisco's side and gently pulled back the dressing on his forehead. "Lucas Tso is seldom wrong, but in this case, it's healed properly. No signs of infection." Ben turned his head to Sunnie. "Perhaps Lucas had the idea you needed to come in to the clinic for some other reason, cousin."

Sunnie looked flustered. It was an interesting view of such a sleek, tough woman.

"Get a sterilized tray from the cabinet behind you," Ben told her. "We'll have those sutures out in no time."

While he waited for Sunnie to tear open sterile wraps and arrange the tray, Cisco spoke to the Brotherhood doctor. "You heard about the body of the old man we found?"

Ben nodded as he took a pointed scissorlike instrument from the tray.

"We also just got ourselves caught in deep snow up in the mountains. It's time for us to stop riding in Sunnie's open Jeep. Do you happen to know if my car's been repaired? Is the garage still open at this hour so I can check?"

"Hold still, will you." Ben held Cisco's head steady with one hand and began snipping the medicinal threads with the other. "Actually, I heard from Junior Gashie this morning. He's had to order a new window for the driver's-side door. No one nearby stocks glass windows like the one that was shot out. He wanted to ask you first, but I guaranteed he would be reimbursed."

"Thanks. Yeah. I'll take care of it. But how much longer will it be?"

"A few days. A week at the most." Ben dropped a few

tiny threads onto the tray and let the scissors drop out of his hand onto it, as well.

"Is there a car rental office near here? I don't want to take any more chances with our safety out in the open."

Sunnie piped up then. "Speak for yourself. I'm fine in the Jeep."

"Oh, yeah, you're just fine turning blue and getting frostbite. You're done riding around in the snow, sugar."

Ben turned to her. "Frostbite? Let me see."

"I'm fine. He's exaggerating." She bristled and backed away from the doctor. "Nothing's wrong with me."

With a quick, resigned shake of his head, Ben turned back to Cisco. "There's a rental agency in Farmington. But I've heard they're usually low on cars this time of year. Certainly there won't be any four-wheel-drive vehicles to rent anywhere around here.

"But I have another idea. My wife has been out in the desert collecting herbs and medicinal plants for the last few weeks, getting ready for the real winter to set in. She had to stop collecting today when the storm came up. For the next few weeks of cold weather, she'll be spending her days inside the Plant Tender's cabin, putting together salves and special herb mixes for the medicine men. She won't need her four-wheel-drive SUV and I'm sure she'd be happy to let Sunnie use it."

"Oh, I couldn't ask her to do that," Sunnie exclaimed.

Ben turned his head and put a hand on her shoulder. "It will be Tory's pleasure. Let us help you, cousin. You can pick up the SUV at the Plant Tender's cabin in the morning."

Cisco saw what might've been the flame of embarrassment on someone else as it added color to Sunnie's face. Then it lit a fire in her eyes. She didn't want anyone's help, he knew. But taking anything from the doctor and his wife seemed especially hard on her.

Too bad. Cisco was determined to keep her out of the elements.

"We'll take the SUV, with thanks," Cisco said as he slid off the table. "Now I have another question. Is there somewhere close where we can get rooms for the night? It's colder than freezing hell out there. There's no way I'm going all the way back to Window Rock in the Jeep tonight."

"The closest motels are in Farmington, I'm afraid," Ben told him. "But if Sunnie can stomach another offer…"

Ben took her by the shoulders. "You look exhausted. In my professional medical opinion, you need to keep out of the open for tonight. Go stay in the mobile home up the road—the one I maintain for nights when I'm working late."

"I know the one," she said. "But you might need it."

Ben smiled at her. "I'm leaving in a few minutes to spend the night at home with my beautiful wife. We haven't seen much of each other lately, what with my patient load and my work for the Brotherhood, and I intend to snuggle down with her in front of the fire for a long winter's night. Take the mobile home."

Sunnie relented after a moment. "All right. Tell Tory we'll be at the Plant Tender's cabin first thing to borrow the SUV."

Ben heaved a deep sigh and shrugged. "Yeah, she'll be at work before dawn. But you don't need to be there quite that early. Wait until the sun's up and it's warmer before you make the trip."

When the doctor left and Sunnie had his keys in hand, Cisco turned to her. "Where's the Plant Tender's cabin?"

Sunnie's eyes were full of storms, her shoulders slumped with fatigue. "Back up in the mountains. Back the same way we came down."

The minute Sunnie stepped out the clinic door into the last light of dusk she felt the shadow of evil creeping around the parking lot. She tensed and stopped, focused on hearing a high-pitched buzz that would mean the Skinwalkers were nearby. She found nothing unusual. Nothing in the darkness to see. Nothing but silence reached her ears.

Then she realized there really were no sounds. None of the normal nocturnal noises of the remote high desert. Where were the night birds and insects? What had happened to the winds?

Chills ran down her arms that had nothing to do with the weather. "Let's go. Ben's mobile home is close. Just turn down the gravel road over there and it's less than a few hundred yards. Directly below Blue Bird Ridge."

"What's up?" Cisco asked. "You look like you're ready for an attack. What do you know that I don't?"

"Nothing. I don't...well, things don't feel right, okay? Just get in and drive. We'll be there in minutes."

Cisco was already wrenching the door open and starting the engine. "I'll take your word for it. Get in!"

He hit the gas and screamed out of the parking lot on two wheels. The Jeep wasn't the most stable vehicle on earth, but Cisco handled it like an expert.

Under his capable hands, the Jeep sprinted around the corner, and gravel sprayed from the tires in a fantail. Sunnie was just about to call herself a foolish neurotic and relax when a huge black SUV loomed out of the darkness and was on their tail in an instant. Cisco flipped the gun out of his coat pocket and dropped it in her lap.

"Use it if you get a chance—if they get close enough," he said without looking at her. "When we get there, I'll take over. We'll need cover."

Picking the gun up and removing the safety, she twisted in her seat to sight the SUV that followed right on their bumper and prepared herself. "I can use a gun as well as you. Just get us there. Ben will have a protective shield around his home. All we have to do is drive into it."

She heard a ping. Then heard another. Oh, hell. The evil one in the SUV was shooting at them, probably trying to blow the tires and stop them before they reached safety. Standing up on the seat, Sunnie braced her knees on the seat back, aimed and fired.

"What the hell? Get down and buckle up!"

"I hit 'em," she screamed over his loud cursing. "They're backing away some."

Cisco reached up, grabbed her one-handed by the waistband of her jeans and threw her back into the seat. "We're here, little Miss Sniper. Give me back the .38. Now!"

Chapter 10

The two of them were still arguing over his weapon as they passed through the shield and unlocked the door to Ben's house. Ducking inside, they slammed it after themselves. Cisco couldn't remember being as scared for anyone in his entire life. He'd been positive she was about to die.

As the fear receded, anger took its place. Good old-fashioned anger that was much easier on his sensibilities.

He hadn't liked having that much adrenaline pumping through his body on someone else's account. So much dread of losing something he hadn't yet found.

He set the .38 on a table, pitched his cap and coat and rounded on her. "Were you trying to commit suicide out there just now?" he asked as coolly as he could manage.

Sunnie flicked on a soft light, turned her back to him and slipped out of her own coat. "It doesn't matter."

"What?" The rage hardened his voice as he reached out and grabbed her shoulder. "You expected to die. You *want* to die?"

She yanked free of his grip. "If I can take one or more of them with me, I'll gladly die for it."

"Not with me along, you won't." He stepped in front of her, kept crowding her when she tried to move away.

"Is this how you convince people to turn themselves in, Bounty Hunter? Bully them?" She shoved at his chest. "Well, it won't work on me. Move out of my way."

"No. You're not hiding this time. Stand still and listen."

He grabbed her arm, swung her up close when she tried to shake him off. Her next move was lightning-fast. Sunnie cracked him hard in the belly with her elbow, and as his breath expelled, she stomped on his foot, then used her back to leverage him up and over her body.

The shame hit him almost as hard as hitting the wood floor did. He didn't normally manhandle women. And this was his second go-round with Sunnie. But as he rubbed against the pain in his gut and looked up into her face, he saw it radiant with the heat of battle. The slender but sturdy woman was not in the least afraid of him, only madder than hell and ready for a fight.

Well, fine. She could damn well join the club.

When she turned slightly to walk away, he grabbed her hand and pulled. At the same time he swept his leg around to knock her off her feet. As she tumbled, he positioned his body under hers and rolled with her so that he was on top and she was pinned beneath him.

"First you want to use me for bait," he growled. "Then you don't care if I die alongside you—just as long as a Skinwalker or two dies with us. Nice."

"You're not my concern. Killing Skinwalkers, killing the Wolf—that's all that matters."

"Like hell. If you think that, you're nothing but a monster like they are." He held her arms down and got right in her face. "You matter," he said in a hoarse whisper. "What's there between us matters."

She closed her eyes and turned her head. For a second he thought she might cry. He'd much rather she give in and talk to him. He backed off slightly. But he hadn't counted on a fake-out.

"There's nothing between us," she roared, flipping him off her and jumping to her feet. "And don't call me names. You have no right. No damned idea what you're talking about."

Cisco heard the guilt in her voice, even as her anger shimmered and bounced off her words. "I have a right," he groaned, preparing himself for round two.

Springing upright, he made a dive for her. The two of them crashed into a coffee table and fell backward onto the couch.

"I don't need this." Her teeth were gritted, her hands fisted. "I don't need you. Back off."

"You *need* to shut up."

Frustrated and pushed farther over a civilized edge than he could remember, Cisco crushed his mouth to hers. The electric shock of her kissing him back, along with the half-formed fantasy that gushed in to replace the anger, had him lifting his head to look down at her in amazed wonder.

"Don't tell me what to do." Grabbing his head with both hands, she jerked him back down to her lips.

Sunnie's brain took a holiday and let passion and heat replace all control. To hell with it. To hell with putting off what they'd both craved.

She didn't care if she died killing Skinwalkers. But she suddenly did care if she died before having sex with this ornery man who sometimes looked at her with rage—but more often looked at her with such sensual ardor that he took her breath away.

It was time to get what she'd hungered for.

And what she wanted…wanted her back. Cisco's mouth was relentless. Hot and mindless with the rush, she dived into his mouth as he opened for her, and their tongues tangled as their bodies and minds had only moments before.

Digging her fingers into his hair, she yanked his head back, then beat on his chest. "Get out of those clothes," she demanded, already out of breath.

He studied her a second, but then reared away and pulled the shirt and sweater over his head in one move. The flesh and hair on his chest was so perfectly masculine, so athletic and dynamic, for a moment she was stunned.

Just enough time for Cisco to reach for the hem of her sweatshirt and rip it over her head. The slightly chilled air touching her heated skin drove her nuts. Shoving at him, she rolled them both off the couch and onto the floor below. She wanted to consume him, needed his body so badly she wanted to shout and cry in sheer desperation.

Straddling him, she raked her nails down the muscles

on his arms hard enough to draw blood. But he didn't
seem to notice any pain as he rose up and ripped her bra
right off her body. The sound of the cloth ripping
spurred her to a higher, crazier plain.

As he clamped his mouth on her breast, she moaned,
letting her head fall back to give him full access. He was
using tongue and teeth, and she panted like an animal
in response. Sucking, blowing heated breaths over her
tender tips, he feasted on her until her brain was aflame
and her body strung impossibly tight. More, she
thought. All of it. Everything. Now.

Collapsing against him, she bit into his shoulder to
stem the curse that threatened to explode from her
mouth. The next thing she knew, she was under him and
he was dragging her boots and jeans off and pitching
them aside.

Cisco was breathing hard, but the breath stilled in his
lungs when he saw her lying perfectly naked below
him. He'd thought there would be one more layer, but
she was suddenly bare to his eyes. And writhing with
desire. He straddled her and bent to take her mouth in
a fierce assault. But when her hips came up and ground
against him, he knew things had to move faster.

Scrambling off, he used one hand to shove his jeans
down his hips while using the other hand to cup her. She
was hot. Wet. Then burning up and drenched as he
probed the fiery spot he'd hungered to touch. A deep,
keening moan left her lips. It was all the sign he'd
needed to move him in a blinding madness to go deeper.

When his fingers entered her core, her eyes rolled
back in her head as the orgasm took her over. It was a

sight like no other and momentarily stopped him. She was beautiful, stunning in her passion.

But she was also wild. In another instant she jerked up and came for him like a tornado. Biting, clawing, crying.

"Now, dammit. I want you inside me now," she begged on a ragged scream.

Losing it all in the raging delusion of pure madness, he pinned her hands above her head and dived right in. She gasped and squirmed. Clenching her legs around his waist, she took him to the hilt. Her urgent madness plunged him headlong into a crimson haze of desire. He bit down on her neck to hold her still, then let his body thrust.

Pounding into her, he drove higher and higher, mindlessly frantic and absent of any hesitations. The crash of release began to thunder in his ears. Cisco raised his head and kept her passion-filled face in sight as both of them exploded in a blast of fiery madness.

As Sunnie caught her breath, she tried to roll out from under Cisco and sit up. But he held on tighter, keeping her pinned beneath his body. Still shuddering in his arms, she felt his primal force reverberating along her nerve endings.

What on earth had she done? She'd certainly never done anything like *that* before. Something had apparently clicked in her brain and driven her a bit mad. Something feral, primitive…savage.

She hadn't given a thought to using protection and especially hadn't considered the consequences. What such an amazing coupling would mean to her in the end.

Trying not to think too much about it now, either,

knowing she was bound to pay a price for forgetting who and what she'd become, Sunnie cleared her throat and found a steady voice.

"Well. That was sure something. But you're crushing me now."

Cisco leaned up on his elbows above her, lessening the strain on her chest. But he remained connected to her. And where they were connected began tingling once again as he stared down into her eyes.

So soon? This would never do.

Lightly touching her shoulder, he murmured, "I bruised you. I...I..."

"I'm fine. You're probably in much worse shape with what I did to you." She wanted to say that she'd never been so wild with anyone before. She wanted to tell him he was only the second man she'd ever been with at all. And that for however long she lived no other man could ever measure up.

But she couldn't. Talking about it seemed pointless. They were not some normal couple who would cuddle and discuss the future after sex. So far, they hadn't even managed to fully discuss their pasts. And tomorrow or the day after, one or both of them would probably be dead.

So whatever had just taken place was an anomaly. A onetime occurrence. Best to leave it at that.

"Are you tired?" he asked as his fingers tenderly touched her cheek. "It's been a helluva day. I think we should talk. But if you'd rather sleep, we can discuss things tomorrow." He smiled at her, ran his thumb over her lips.

"Don't know about you," she mumbled, trying not to notice what his fingers were doing to her, "but I don't need that much sleep. And I can't imagine what we would talk about, anyway."

He took a breath. "We just had unprotected sex. I don't usually do that sort of thing. I want to know how you feel about it."

"No sweat. It's not important. I don't want to discuss feelings. I can't. Feelings tend to make you sloppy. I'd rather not feel anything at all, thank you just the same."

This time he grinned down at her. "So…" His fingers ringed a nipple. "You're not feeling this, then?" He rolled the tip with his thumb and forefinger.

Bending his head, he took the other nipple between his teeth and tugged. The sensation shot between her legs, and a tiny bead of sweat leaked down her temple.

His chin came up as his eyes searched hers. "Or that?"

He caught the bead of sweat with a finger and looked concerned. "All sweaty?"

"Uh…"

Moving faster than the electricity zinging in her veins, Cisco stood up and plucked her off the floor. Before she knew what hit her, he'd swung her up in his arms and headed down the hall.

"I'd guess Ben has a shower in this place. Let's see if it's big enough for two."

Sunnie shrieked and kicked out at air. "Cheater. I can't get decent leverage. Put me down."

"Don't want to wrestle, *mi amor.* I have something else in mind. Relax."

The shower stall was plenty big enough for two, Cisco was pleased to note. He kept her close to his chest while he turned on the taps and adjusted the temperature. No cold showers for them this night.

"I don't need a…"

He cut her words off by crushing his mouth on hers. The flame of her lips brought the heat back to his blood. She lifted her head, drew in a startled breath and kissed him back. Her arms went around his shoulders as she wiggled, trying to get closer.

Stepping into the shower with her still in his arms, Cisco turned his back to the heated water spray and let her slowly slide down his body. Chest to breast, then lower still as he bent to set her feet on solid surface.

"I think we're in need of some soap here, *míja*."

Keeping one hand busy steadying her, he reached for a bar of soap with the other. He moved aside just enough to let the shower water splash her body. She closed her eyes to the spray, and he took the opportunity to run the soap bar over her chest, making her slick and sudsy and delectable. Mmm.

He leaned her up against the tile at the end of the stall so he could use both hands on her. Sliding the bar down her belly, he watched the expression on her face turn from wary and tense to relaxed and sensual. Not able to stand just watching and not tasting, he inched closer, capturing her mouth again as his hands and the soap moved lower.

Soap went into every crevice, teasing, cajoling, incensing, while the hot water set torches of desire to every place it flowed. He reached over to smear soap up her neck, but she was quicker and captured his hand. She dropped the soap and drew his fingers toward her lips, slipping his forefinger inside her mouth. And then she sucked. Sucked his finger in deep while all the while she kept her dreamy, sexy eyes trained on his.

It was quite possibly the most erotic thing that had ever happened to him.

If he'd wondered about her mood or readiness, all such thoughts flew out of his brain. In fact, every single thought disappeared, leaving him nothing but a mass of quivering need.

Pulling his finger free, Cisco slid both his hands under her hips and lifted. "Hold on with your legs," he managed. "Around my waist."

She did and he entered her in one mighty move. He pressed her back against the tile to steady them both. When she moaned and dropped her head, he propelled himself deep inside her.

He nipped his way along her jawline and down her neck as she moaned louder.

"Now. Now," she stuttered through the haze budding around them.

The sounds of her pleading drove liquid fire pulsing through every part of his body. Every inch burned with need and pure pleasure. He felt the sting of her fingernails as she clutched at his shoulders, but there was no pain. Her touch only added fuel to the flames.

Trembling and too near his own release, he waited until he felt the shudder begin rumbling through her again. He thrust deeper as her body began tightening. This time his own moans echoed off the shower walls right along with hers as they followed the same path.

It took him a few seconds to begin breathing again, but when he did, he loosened his grip and let her ease down his body until she seemed steady. He flipped off the water while steam fogged the bathroom. Pulling a towel off the bar, he wrapped her up tight and kept her close.

Then he lifted her off her feet again and went in search of a bed.

When Cisco awakened to morning sun, he was smiling. Until…he turned to find Sunnie not in bed beside him. It had been a short night. But one of his best.

Though he felt her absence as though he'd lost an arm, he lay there a second, telling himself to tread carefully here. Last night he'd misplaced his perspective. In fact, he must've lost his freakin' mind.

Unprotected sex with a woman he didn't know well had been totally unexpected. Especially since there were still a few condoms in foil packs waiting in his pants pocket. He had figured from the start they would end up having sex. And had been prepared. But he'd never imagined he would lose himself entirely to such hot sweaty desire.

But he had. Lost himself. And now he wondered if he could ever again find the person he'd once been.

Or if he even wanted to.

As a young man, he'd changed his life. Gone from a kid buffeted and bruised by family circumstances to an adult who needed no one. An adult who wanted no ties and shunned everything that might remind him of his bitter and embattled youth. He'd had no family, no friends. His employees were loyal but not friends. No one close that might disappoint him as his own parents had. He'd come to the decision long ago that he wanted things to always be that way.

Now he was beginning to feel a connection to Sunnie. One like he had never known before. At first he'd thought the odd emotional link to her was just some misplaced sense of being her guardian. She seemed so all alone and in dire need of someone to stand beside her during her fight.

Since waking up from the lust-filled night, he was seeing things in a different light. He'd quit envisioning his own life as an unbroken line of solitary days and inconsequential nights. But where life went from here was still unclear. After being inside her, after the first taste, he'd felt as though a curtain had been lifted—but only high enough to give him a peek at what might lay beyond.

He needed to step back from this edge of the unknown—and from her. For long enough at least to let these strange sensations begin to sink in. The only thing he couldn't, wouldn't, step back from was the possibility that he and Sunnie had created a new life during their crazy night of lust. But he needed to let that play out. Let Sunnie be the one to take the lead there.

Scrubbing a hand across the thick stubble on his face, Cisco left the bed and headed for another shower. Distance and time to think was what he really needed. Unfortunately it was also imperative that he stick with Sunnie now. She was heading for big trouble. Last night had shown him that much. She didn't have the sense to know when to duck.

And as much as he wished for some space, the need to keep her safe was stronger than ever.

Sunnie stood by the toaster, waiting for the bread to pop. She'd made coffee. But that and toast were the extent of her culinary breakfast talents. Hearing the shower running, she knew it wouldn't be long before Cisco appeared in the kitchen.

Then what?

What would they say to each other? She'd rather not talk about what had happened last night. It had been amazing. Confusing. She'd expected sex between them to be beyond anything she'd ever experienced— and it had been.

But she hadn't expected to feel…joy. There was no other way to describe this feeling. How could something like that have happened? She'd been working so hard to suppress her sorrow and grief, to become numb. But joy had snuck in and captured her spirit when she'd been otherwise occupied.

How could she explain it to herself, let alone to Cisco? She couldn't. Wouldn't.

She didn't want this…this…lightness in her mind. It was almost like stepping out from the shade and being blinded by sunlight.

Damn him, anyway. Darkness and its sister Disaster were the tools she'd been using to keep her edge. Somehow she needed to get that edge back. So Cisco Santiago had just better not expect a soft, cuddly morning from her.

"Good morning," he said in that impossibly sexy voice as he strode into the kitchen. "You made coffee. You're an angel."

An *angel?* Certainly not in this lifetime. And since Navajo tradition didn't include belief in an afterlife, she would likely not be receiving her wings anytime soon.

"I'm making toast, if you want to join me."

"Sure." He sat down at the tiny kitchen counter and studied her. "You're up early. And I see you've pushed back all the window coverings to let the sunshine in. I'm glad to see the sun again, but do you think the Skinwalkers are still outside the house? Will they be waiting to ambush us as we come out?"

She shrugged a shoulder. "They might have been. But I called Hunter Long this morning and he promised to send someone to check it out. The Brotherhood knows how to get rid of any of evil ones that might've been willing to brave the daylight."

Sunnie hadn't even noticed the curtains were pulled back. Why had she done that? Leaving them drawn and the house in shadows was much more like her normal self.

"Also, there's another way for us to leave without being seen," she continued as his toast popped and she put it on a plate before him. "A back way that will get us up in the mountains faster. Without a snowstorm it should be a cinch."

"Good. The sooner we get started, the sooner you'll be out of that open Jeep. I've been thinking…"

"It's not *me* the Skinwalkers are trying to ambush. I've already told you they think I'm dead."

"Yes, you have. But I was thinking more along the lines of ravages of weather."

"Don't worry about me and cold weather. I can take it. In fact, I can take it and still cause plenty of trouble."

"You can say that again," Cisco muttered under his breath.

Chapter 11

Sunnie crept just beyond the invisible line drawn around Ben's mobile home to keep out the Skinwalkers. Standing perfectly still, she sniffed the air and listened for any disturbance. Nothing. Whoever had been stalking them was obviously gone.

"It's cool," she said to Cisco, who was waiting right outside the door. "We should be good to go."

Saying nothing but with an irritated scowl on his face, Cisco gathered up their few things, dumped them in the Jeep and slid in behind the wheel. Sunnie buckled herself in the passenger seat and folded her arms over her waist.

If he was going to be all annoyed again just because she hadn't wanted to be warm and fuzzy this morning, then so be it. At the moment she wanted nothing more from him than a silent drive to the Plant Tender's cabin.

She directed him out the back way and leaned against the seat back as they passed the ginger-colored hills she had loved as a child. Turning left, they drove down a gravel road that skirted a goat farmer's fields. The sun, sparkling against leftover patches of snow, dazzled her eyes, so she flipped on her sunglasses. Still, the colors of her homeland seemed brighter this morning, almost the same as they had when she'd been a kid.

The purple sage looked nearly magenta in the sun's glow. The junipers and piñons gleamed in shades of emerald instead of their usual sage-gray. The broom snakeweed still had blooms of brilliant gold that by all rights of nature should've been long gone by November. Even the coat of the small black goat they drove past was a shiny ebony color today.

All the images and colors were surreal to her, as if she'd been living under a cloud for most of her life. Where was the hazy filtered sunlight of regular mornings?

They left the grazing land and headed up the rocky foothills of the Chuska range. The sky was cobalt-blue with puffy white clouds in a dotted pattern, seemingly spaced in particular designs across the heavens.

"What's that?" Cisco asked as he pointed off to their right.

"The Hogback?" She turned to look at the jagged peaks of sand and rock resembling the spine of a razorback hog.

"Did someone build it like that? And if so, why?"

"Those shapes were designed by nature. Wind and erosion take the top layers of soil and sand and leave those steeply tilted feldspar and sandstone peaks."

"Hey, geologist. To me it looks like a dinosaur was buried there and just the spiny back is protruding."

Sunnie laughed at his images. "Every kid who goes to school around here learns about the geology of the place. It's hard not to. But I didn't know you had such a fanciful bent, Bounty Hunter. In my opinion, it looks like a row of sentinels, standing guard for the Dine against the plundering hordes of time and weather."

The sound of her laughter sent waves of hot, sweet silk down to settle in Cisco's gut. He forgot about being annoyed and managed a smile at her image of soldiers. It was just as fanciful as his dinosaur had been. Yet hers was absolutely right for her. Whatever had made her this way, sentinels and war were a part of Sunnie's life.

It made him wonder what he could do to give her a break from thinking and breathing Brotherhood and Skinwalkers. She was so strong and did her best to stay tough, even managing to convince herself that she didn't care whether she lived or died. But he'd seen the purplish smudges under her eyes and noted the bleak look. No one who didn't care about living could possess as much passion as she'd shown last night. He didn't buy it for one minute.

"I guess I haven't told you yet why I'm investigating that old murder," he said before he thought it through. He'd wanted to take her mind off war, but now the spotlight would be thrust at him.

She tilted her chin. "No. You haven't."

No turning back now. He would have to tell her the story. But maybe this would be for the best. There were times when he needed someone to confide in. And she came from the reservation and knew the people involved.

"I'm doing it to fulfill my mother's last wish."

"Oh? Well, that's good. Then you'll have a kind of closure, right?"

He shook his head but didn't turn away from the road ahead. "So far, the investigation has only brought up more questions than answers. Questions I could've done without."

"That's a shame. But what was your mother's wish?"

"She wanted to know what really happened to my father and why he never returned to us."

"Well, it's good that you—oh. You think the murdered man was your father?"

"I know he was."

Sunnie reached over and tenderly laid a hand on his arm. "Researching the old facts of his death must be hell for you. Are you positive the dead man was your father?"

Nodding, Cisco swallowed back any leftover emotion and began the tale of what he'd learned. "I'd never known my father's last name. He supported us and showed up now and then, but he never stayed long. When he disappeared for good, it changed our whole lives. After Mother died never learning what happened to him, I went to visit her sister in Mexico. That's where I found his last name and that he'd worked for the U.S. government. My mother had written it in a letter."

Sunnie made no comment, but he knew her mind was whirling with questions. And *the* answer she wanted was the hardest one to say.

"Apparently," Cisco began again slowly, "my father

had been employed as what's known as a 'disguise master' for the U.S. Marshals Service. He built new images for people in the Witness Security Program and was supposedly the best at his job.

"But he quit suddenly one day," Cisco added. "Told his supervisors that he was moving with the family back to his wife's homeland on the Navajo reservation."

"You said your mother was from Mexico. Was he lying?"

Cisco took a deep breath. "No. He was never married to my mother. We were not the family he'd meant."

"You mean…" She shook her head and turned to look out the windshield. "I really am sorry. That must've been a difficult fact for you to learn."

"It was. But the worst was yet to come. When I found the articles in the paper about his murder, there were pictures of his Navajo widow and grieving children."

"Children? You have siblings you didn't even know you had? Are they still on the reservation?"

He nodded but couldn't bring himself to say it.

"Have you called them? Told them?"

When he said nothing, Sunnie's eyes took on a panicked expression. "What was your father's name?"

With a deep sigh he said, "Sam Long."

"Oh. My. God. That's why I remembered hearing something about the murder. And that's why you acted so strangely to the name Long. Hunter and Kody Long are your half brothers."

After the worst news was out in the open, the two of them fell into a sullen silence. Cisco knew she would want to know more and could just hear her thoughts nagging him to tell Hunter and Kody who he really was. Tough. He wasn't ready yet. He wasn't even sure now that he should've told her.

It didn't take them half an hour more to reach the other side of the mountain range and the wooded cliffs and meadows where the Plant Tender's cabin was located. It was a much easier climb than coming down the day before in the snowstorm had been.

Sunnie directed him to pull up in front and stop. "Don't get out of the Jeep just yet," she advised. "In Navajo tradition we wait to be recognized and invited in."

"But I thought Ben's wife was non-Navajo. An outsider, like me."

She nodded. "Tory came to the reservation without knowing the traditions, that's true. But she's had a couple of years of immersion and training in the Navajo Way. She's the New Plant Tender and should be treated with the respect of her position."

He nodded but didn't really get it. Still, if Sunnie wanted to wait for an invitation, they would wait in the Jeep.

Minutes went by, but nothing happened. Sunnie began rubbing her arms as though she were getting colder.

"What if Mrs. Wauneka isn't here?"

Sunnie shook off the suggestion. "I saw her SUV beside the cabin as we pulled up. Ben said she would be waiting."

They sat another few minutes in silence.

"Tory used to live in this cabin," Sunnie told him. "Back before she and Ben got married. The Old Plant

Tender left it to her after she died. Maybe Tory's in the shower or on the phone or something."

"Maybe." Cisco was getting a bad feeling about this. "Are you sensing anything strange? Any Skin-walker vibes?"

She shook her head. "No. But I agree things don't seem right. The cabin must have a Brotherhood circle of protection around it. They would never leave the Plant Tender and her place unprotected. Still…"

Looking toward the cabin with the first real sense of foreboding he'd seen on her face, Sunnie continued, "Maybe we should at least go knock on the door. What if she's fallen and broken something and can't get up?"

Cisco climbed out of the Jeep and went around to Sunnie's side as she eased out of her seat, too. "How old is she?"

"In her late thirties."

"Healthy?"

"Very."

"Then it's unlikely that she's sick or injured." He took Sunnie's hand and pulled his .38 from his jacket pocket. "If something goes down in there, you need to act fast. Do what I tell you. If I say run, run like hell."

"All right."

Cisco was surprised to hear Sunnie agreeing so easily to his instructions. She must be really afraid for her friend. It made him even more nervous than before. He had a moment, one second, when he fervently wished Sunnie was armed. She could protect herself just fine. But it was too late now to do anything about it.

The intensity of the situation escalated when they

reached the cabin's front stoop. There were no sounds, not inside the cabin nor from the surrounding forest.

Sunnie dropped his hand and knocked on the door. Nothing. Then she tried the knob and found the door open.

She opened her mouth to call out, but Cisco laid a hand on her shoulder to keep her quiet. "No noise," he whispered. "I'll go first."

"But…"

He shot a warning glare in her direction and took a half step inside. Sunnie was right on his heels. He eased behind the front door and dragged her flat against the wall with him. If they were going to search this cabin, they'd do it right. Like shadows.

Listening for any sounds, he didn't hear so much as the murmur of an electric clock or a computer. Nothing seemed out of place in the living room, but it was difficult to judge with all the plants strewn around on nearly every surface.

"Where is she?" Sunnie murmured with panic rising in her voice.

Taking it one room at a time, Cisco carefully led the way, winding around the cabin. Nothing seemed overturned as if there had been a struggle. Every room, every leaf, was perfect. It looked as if the occupant had just stepped away for a moment and would soon return.

When they got to the kitchen, the first thing they spotted was the back door standing wide-open. "Oh, thank goodness," Sunnie said. "She must be out back gathering plants or herbs. Let's go call her."

She dashed out the door before he could stop her. He followed behind, but slowly. Things were still all wrong.

"Hold it," he said when Sunnie began calling out and walking toward the woods. "Just how far does this invisible protective line extend around the house?"

Turning back to him, Sunnie smiled. "About fifty feet. But there aren't any Skinwalkers around here. I'd know if they were waiting. You can hear it. Come on. I want to find Tory."

He caught up to her and grabbed her by the hand again. "Slow down. Things aren't right. Don't you feel it? Let's not rush off and make trouble for ourselves."

"But…"

Just then, a loud shriek from a large bird came from above their heads. Sunnie immediately froze and looked up.

When she spotted a benign circling hawk, her breathing came easier. It was not a Skinwalker raven or vulture getting ready to attack them. But as she stared at the raptor for a moment, she realized the bird was trying to tell them something. This must be one of the Brotherhood's Bird People allies. But what was it trying to say?

"What's going on?" Cisco asked.

He was so close that she felt the heat from his body and could even feel the shimmering tension in his muscles.

"Uh…" How to tell him about Bird People? "That hawk seems to want us to follow. Maybe it can lead us to Tory."

"You're kidding. You want to follow a bird? Like a dog or something? How?"

The hawk began circling lower and lower. Low enough to fly below the tree limbs.

"Son of a bitch," Cisco said with a shake of his head.

"Okay, but you keep low, too. I don't like any part of this. It's too weird."

Within another fifty feet the trees began to close in around them. Still the bird winged ahead of them, staying just in sight.

The hawk finally landed in the low-hanging branch of a ponderosa pine. Sunnie raced to the spot below it.

As she noticed one of Tory's protected herb gardens, her stomach flipped over. Every plant had been crushed and the muddy dirt from the melting snow was trampled with deep scrapes and prints.

"No. Oh, no. Tory, what's happened to you?" she called out to her absent friend as she fell to her knees.

Squeezing her eyes shut, Sunnie could see Tory's smiling face in her mind. The image of the last time they'd been together as Tory laughed and joked about Sunnie's recovery from the Skinwalker attack was as clear as if it had been yesterday. Tory was so caring, so giving. She'd always believed that Sunnie could be cured of anything and had made being injured almost fun with her sarcastic wisecracks and tender touches. Tory was the first real friend Sunnie had ever known.

How could anything bad happen to her?

Cisco reached Sunnie's side, laid a steady hand on her arm and bent down to study the ground. He knelt in the dirt, inspecting the scene. What he found made him stiffen his back. Blood. Not enough to mean someone had been murdered here but enough to mean someone had put up a fight on this spot.

"I don't think she's dead," he told Sunnie softly. "It looks like they surprised her here and took her away. I believe she struggled with them, but I don't believe they killed her."

"What?" Sunnie raised her head and he saw the shock in her eyes. "She can't be dead. Not her. She can't…."

Cisco draped his arm around her shoulders and pulled her close. "No, there's not enough blood evidence, only enough for a scuffle. I'm sure she wasn't killed here. But they've taken her for some reason."

Sunnie pushed him away and broke down then. Just bent in two and crumbled over in a heap, sobbing hysterically and pounding her fists into the dirt.

It was a sight he never would've believed. The strong woman sniper. The tough but sexy-as-hell female to whom he'd felt such a link. He'd even spilled secrets to her he hadn't intended to tell anyone. Now she was a solitary, scared woman worried about her friend.

His heart ached for her. Her tears drove nails into his gut and messed with his brain. He wanted to soothe her fears, but he wasn't sure she would let him.

Cisco looked around them then and noticed the hawk had already gone. There was no one nearby and not the slightest noise nor breath of air. All of a sudden he didn't like the idea of being out here in the forest and so exposed.

"Let's get you back inside," he said as he gently lifted her in his arms. Damn. He couldn't stand seeing her weak like this. It was killing him.

Carrying her back to the cabin, Cisco's mind raced with ways to help Sunnie's friend. Anything to get his Sunnie back. He actually knew the best way, but his spirit still resisted.

By the time they entered the kitchen again and he'd slammed the door behind them, he was shaky as hell and ready to kill someone in order to put things right. He gently lowered her into a chair at the kitchen table.

Sunnie's tough veneer came back in an instant. She popped right back up and stood toe-to-toe with him.

"You're the bounty hunter," she said as she smacked him in the chest. "You find people. Find Tory."

A tiny niggle of relief about her being back in control snuck into his mind. He had to stifle the grin he felt.

The smile was fairly easy to hide, but his hands moved without his permission. Before he knew it, he'd buried one hand in her hair. Cupping the back of her neck with the other, he hauled her tightly to him.

"You're damn straight that's what I do," he said with a hoarse cough. "We'll find her, *mija*. But you have to stay strong."

She leaned her head against his chest and sighed. "Help me."

Those words undid him. He buried his face in her hair and babbled tender, soothing Spanish in her ear. *"Si, si. Mi amor…"*

Sunnie pulled back to stare up at him. Looking into her eyes, he became so flustered he couldn't think of anything to say. So he let his lips do the talking in a desperate, aggressive kiss.

A moment later he lifted his head and pushed her away just as aggressively. "Dammit all to hell. I let you get to me. Like never before. Stop that."

"Cisco, stop what? What did I…?"

He backed away when she stepped closer. "Quiet,"

he growled in a whisper. "Just keep quiet. I have to think."

She fisted her hands but left them at her sides. Too bad. He was itching to go a few more rounds.

There seemed no way out now. He was going to have to do what he'd dreaded.

Dismal and grim-faced, he reached into a pocket and took out both his cell phone and Hunter's card. After vowing to stay out of his half brothers' way while in Navajoland, it was time to suck it up and admit defeat. Cisco had little choice but to give in and call the Brotherhood for help.

Nearly half an hour later Sunnie heard a car door slam and stepped out on the porch to wave in Kody Long and Michael Ayze. She'd known Cisco was not eager to talk to Hunter again. Lucky for him, Hunter was not the brother who'd arrived. Now she had to decide how to go about introducing Cisco to his other brother.

"*Ya'at'eeh*," Michael said. "May we step inside?"

She nodded.

Kody spoke up and said, "Mind if I head out back first? I'd like to see the scene of the kidnapping for myself. Maybe there will be some clues to where they've taken her." He disappeared around the side of the house.

Sunnie nearly collapsed with relief at having the Brotherhood involved in finding Tory. They would know what to do. Michael stepped through the threshold, and she introduced the brilliant professor to Cisco.

"So how do you fit into all this?" Michael asked Cisco almost immediately.

"I don't fit into the kidnapping. I came here with Sunnie to borrow Tory Wauneka's SUV. We discovered her missing. Called the Brotherhood to help."

"What did you need the Plant Tender's SUV for? What are you doing on the rez?"

Sunnie didn't know for sure what Cisco would say. Michael was not his relative, but still. Saying too much might cause him more trouble and more questions than he wanted to handle right now.

"I'm here investigating an old, cold murder. And after driving through a snowstorm, Sunnie and I needed better transportation. Dr. Ben offered. We took him up on it."

Michael gave him a strange look.

"The investigation is on hold for now," Cisco added quickly. "I intend to do whatever I can to help locate Sunnie's friend before going on with anything else."

"We haven't told Ben about his wife's disappearance yet," Michael told them. "We wanted to make sure…"

At that moment Kody came through the kitchen door in a rage. "It was Skinwalkers, all right. The place is still vibrating like crazy." He rounded on Cisco with his hands fisted. "You're the bounty hunter we've heard about. Just what the hell is going on with you? First there's Shorty Tom left mutilated in his own paddock. Now the Plant Tender gets taken right out of her own protected cabin. What kind of evil have you brought down on us?"

Sunnie stepped between the two half brothers. She'd made the decision to let Cisco tell both Hunter and Kody about their relationship. It wasn't any of her business. But she couldn't let anyone accuse Cisco unjustly.

"None of that was his doing," she blasted at Kody. "He's not a Skinwalker and you know it. This cabin is protected, and he couldn't even take a step inside the door if he was one of the evil ones."

Kody didn't back down. "If they didn't murder her on the spot, they must want something," he muttered to Cisco over Sunnie's head. "I'm guessing you know what that is, stranger."

Cisco put a hand on her shoulder and gently pushed her to one side. "That's jumping to some pretty big conclusions, even for a fed." He stood within an arm's length of his own half brother and looked about ready to take a swing.

Sunnie was gearing up to jump in between them again when Michael's phone rang.

He answered and then the expression on his face froze in a sober mask. Answering the caller in Navajo, he said a few words Sunnie couldn't make out and then handed the phone over to Kody.

Michael turned to them. "Dr. Ben has just been contacted by the Skinwalkers."

"Contacted? How?"

"I don't have all the details, but we now know why they wanted Tory—to trade her life for my knowledge."

Sunnie felt herself go limp and reached out to grab Cisco's steady arm. He stepped closer and put his arm around her waist.

The move was not missed by Michael, but the Navajo professor said nothing about it. "I must go to my office at the college. A package will be delivered with copies of the ancient parchments the Brotherhood has been looking for—but that the Skinwalkers apparently found first."

Michael stopped, dragged in a breath. "If I can translate them within the next three days, we'll get Tory back unharmed."

They all looked at each other. Sunnie finally asked the question.

"And what if you can't?"

Chapter 12

Kody Long hung up Michael's phone and stepped to Sunnie's side. "He will." Kody's eyes gentled and filled with compassion. "Michael can do anything. Have no fear."

Cisco had not expected such a soft look from the tough FBI agent. As Kody murmured more words of comfort, Cisco studied his half brother. The eye color was not the same as Hunter's, and that meant it wasn't the same as his own or their father's, either. But if Cisco remembered right, the hair and skin coloring was a match to their father. It felt odd seeing such family resemblance in a man he'd never met before.

Sunnie turned her head to address Michael. "Did I have something to do with this kidnapping? The Skinwalkers have been following us for a couple of days.

Did I lead them here? Is it my fault the Skinwalkers took Tory?"

Cisco tightened his grip around her waist and felt her straighten at his touch.

Michael shook his head and held out his hand in a placating gesture. "It's no one's fault. They needed some advantage to make me do whatever they desire. None of us, least of all Tory, would've thought that stepping outside our protective circle for a few minutes in the daylight would lead to such a drastic result. I'm sure she's done it many times before today and has always been safe.

"And by the way," Michael continued, "this isn't the first occasion where they've kidnapped an innocent in order to force the Brotherhood to their will. We beat them the last two times and we'll do it again for the Plant Tender."

Kody had taken Sunnie's hand, but now he dropped it and stepped back. "We must go. Michael has much to do, and the rest of the Brotherhood will be busy working on our own ways to find out where they've taken Tory."

Kody remained still for a moment, standing as he was and gazing down at Sunnie, until he finally said, "You two should stay here in the Plant Tender's cabin for a few nights. If the Skinwalkers are still looking for one of you, they won't be expecting you in her cabin. Not since the kidnapping. It'll be the last place they look.

"Tory would want it that way," Kody added. "Use her SUV as you planned. I'll bet the keys are on her desk or on the kitchen counter."

Sunnie shook her head but never uttered a sound.

"Do this, little cousin," Michael insisted gently. "Stay safe so I can be free to concentrate on the translations."

Sunnie lifted her chin. "You won't actually give the Skinwalkers the secret to everlasting life, will you?"

Michael's lips turned up in a soft, sad smile. "I must believe there'll be another way in the end. Nonetheless, I'll still make the translations. It may be our only leverage for getting Tory back."

The Brotherhood men left, satisfied Sunnie would be safe enough inside the cabin. Cisco tried to tell himself it was for the best that he hadn't said anything to Kody about their combined heritage. Now was not a good time to bring up sensitive and potentially volatile subjects that probably had nothing to do with Skinwalkers.

At that thought, though, Cisco stopped himself. Why *had* the Skinwalkers been so interested in him? Was it just because he'd been asking odd questions? That didn't sit right. What was it about an old murder that had captured the Skinwalkers' attention?

Without more digging into the Skinwalkers, the whole investigation would end here. Cisco had never been a quitter. But he was not able to protect Sunnie and still concentrate on his father's murderer. He would just have to let the problem gel in his mind for a while.

"But I don't need protecting, Bounty Hunter." Sunnie was so furious she was shimmering with rage. "You know I can take care of myself. I can't just hang out and do nothing to help Tory.

"Are you coming back to the scene of the kidnapping

with me now or not?" Sunnie twisted her arm free of Cisco's grip and headed for the kitchen door.

She wasn't positive he would follow. But she hoped he would. In the hour since the Brotherhood had left the cabin she'd drunk enough coffee to float a ship and had listened to Cisco talk about finding deadbeat felons until she was numb. It was time for her to move.

He reached her before she could set foot out the door. "Slow down. I thought you wanted to help find your friend. Let's not jump off the cliff in a suicide pact." Spinning her around to face him, he loomed over her. "As a matter of fact, I distinctly remember you agreeing to do what I say…to follow my lead."

"That was before—" Sunnie couldn't bring herself to say it: before they knew Tory had been taken. The idea of her friend being held by those rat bastards for even a few seconds was almost more than Sunnie could bear.

Rallying in the face of Cisco's stern look, she pressed her point. "And you promised you'd find her if I stayed strong." She shoved her elbow into his chest and followed up with a light punch to the gut. "That strong enough for you?"

Cisco huffed out a breath but only narrowed his eyes.

"Terrific," she said, then rolled her own eyes. "Stay here if you want. But I'm going back into the woods to see if Kody missed anything. He was so furious and afraid for Tory that I don't think he gave the scene enough study."

"He's a fed, *mija.* They're trained to look for clues. What kind of training have you had?"

"Training in control," she muttered through gritted

teeth. "I've taught myself to stalk prey through deserts and over rocks, finding signs that most investigators would overlook. I've sat for twelve hours at a time without moving so much as an eyelash, waiting. Waiting for the one right shot that never came. My training in self-discipline is as good as, if not better than, the FBI's best crime-scene class."

Cisco folded his arms and shook his head. "Oh, yeah, your patience must be legendary. We've been here alone in the cabin since the Brotherhood left for—what?—a whole hour? And you can't even manage to sit still for that long."

"I'm going." Screw him. If he wanted to cower here in the kitchen, let him. "I'd hoped you would be my backup and cover me. But since you don't want to go back out there, how about letting me take the .38?"

He opened his mouth and snarled as if he would say something she didn't want to hear. But then he snapped his lips closed again and drew the gun from his waistband.

"Fine," he growled, low and furious. "We'll go together. But we're going to take it slow. Stay close."

"Fine." Sunnie let go of the breath she'd been holding as she stormed out the door ahead of him and quickly moved into the woods.

Cisco tried to keep his temper in check. Coming out here to the scene of the kidnapping would let Sunnie get rid of some of her excess energy. He could think of better ways of doing that, of course. But then, he'd promised himself not to resort to easy ways of distracting her.

Unless she suggested them first. He'd wanted her to

think of the same distractions as had been deviling him ever since they'd been alone again. His body was certainly up for a good tussle—and all the erotic physical things that would inevitably come after that with the two of them.

"What are you doing?" he called out as she stalked away from the Plant Tender's herb garden. "Stay where I can see you."

She turned. "I know Kody figures the Skinwalkers used their superhuman powers to fly Tory out of the woods. But that would mean carrying her. She's not fat or anything, but she's no lightweight, either. I think I've spotted extra-large paw prints leading away from the scene. Come see what you think."

"Tracking prints is not exactly my strong suit, you know. Now if this were a series of hidden bank accounts, I'd be your man."

She tsked and then darted behind a tree where he couldn't see her. Damn woman would be the death of him yet. No doubt *literally* his absolute living end.

He exhaled and went after her. But he hadn't gone two steps when something on the ground caught his eye. Off to the side of the trail Sunnie had been following was a patch of melting snow. Though the sun was high in the sky, this patch had so far been protected by the huge ponderosa pines towering above it. Right in the middle of the white ice crystals he spotted the tip of something blue peeking out from underneath. Dark blue. Not a color normally found in snow or the dirt below it.

Nudging the off-color object with his toe, Cisco expected to find a scarf or some other piece of clothing that the Plant Tender had been wearing when she'd been snatched. He was right in the middle of arguing with himself about mentioning such a find to Sunnie at all when a small blue notebook appeared at the tip of his boot.

Cisco bent to pick it up, then straightened and called out, "Hey, Miss Patience and Self-Control, come back here a second. I've found something."

While he flipped through the pages of the notebook, the sound of Sunnie's footsteps through the dense brush soothed his nerves. Within a few minutes she was close enough that he could hear her breathing hard.

"What is it?" she asked, out of breath, as she sidled up beside him and tried to see what he held in his hands.

"It's a notebook. But the entries are in code."

"Is that what all those squiggles are? Some sort of code?"

"Yeah. I've studied tons of encryption methods in order to chase money around the world, finding recalcitrant felons and their hordes of cash. I've also written my own code a time or two."

Sunnie continued to stare at the book as though she expected to see the answer to where her friend had been taken written at the top of each page.

"Navajos are famous for our code-talkers," she murmured almost to herself. "They saved many U.S. forces during World War II. But that code was done in the spoken word. The Dine haven't had a written language for very long."

"Do you think this might belong to the Plant Tender, then?" Cisco asked. "Something she kept in order to help her identify plants and their locations?"

She looked more carefully at the strange shapes and

designs. "No way. Besides being the Plant Tender, Tory's also a medical doctor. There's no chance she would make tiny, tidy marks like those. When we worked together, her handwriting was easy to decipher. But at the same time, it was typically sloppy."

"You're sure, then? This book could not belong to Tory."

Sunnie shook her head and looked up at him. "Should we call the Brotherhood and tell them we found this?"

"What would they do with it?"

"You're right," she agreed without even hearing his argument. "Michael is a trained symbologist. He could break the code. But we know he's busy translating parchments for the Skinwalkers. You are probably better at doing something like this than any of the other Brotherhood members."

"Then—what?" Cisco asked rhetorically. "We keep it for at least tonight and I give it a shot? It's possible that, given enough time, I'll be able to decipher at least a few pages."

Sunnie shrugged an acknowledgment that keeping it was probably the only course to take.

"Okay. I guess that's what we'll do." Cisco looked around the area, trying to decide which step to take next. Copper-colored streaks lined with gold and rose spilled across the sky above them. Almost dusk in these hills, it would soon be too dark to see. Time to head back inside.

And go to work.

A few minutes later Cisco was in the Plant Tender's office, hunched over Tory's computer. Sunnie was rummaging around in the kitchen's shelves, looking for something to eat. She hadn't been hungry for weeks. Now all of a sudden, when there was no food around, she was starved.

She'd barely gotten a chance to warm up after being outside and to decide what kind of canned food to open when a sound came from out front. A traditional Navajo had apparently arrived and awaited permission to visit.

Sunnie walked to the front window and carefully peeked out the side of the curtains. She recognized the truck but could scarcely believe her eyes.

Audrey Long—Kody and Hunter Long's mother, now remarried and called Mrs. James—sat in the passenger seat, watching the door for a signal. Why would she come here? Sunnie knew she lived close by. But had anyone told her the Plant Tender had been kidnapped?

Sunnie opened the front door and waved the older woman inside. This situation felt so strange. The woman who had been married to Cisco's father was coming for a visit. Sunnie almost turned to call out to Cisco but changed her mind and decided to wait until she knew more.

"Ya'at'eeh," Mrs. James said as she came close. Her arms were loaded with plastic containers and tinfoil-covered plates. "My son tells me you and the outsider will be staying here for a few days. I worried that the Plant Tender's kitchen would not have been supplied in anticipation of guests."

"You brought food? Wow." Sunnie took over some of Mrs. James's burden and led the way to the kitchen. "Who drove you over?" Sunnie asked. "Would whoever it is like to come in?"

"My new husband was kind enough to drive this old woman. He prefers to wait. I've told him I will not stay too long."

Cisco appeared at the kitchen doorway. "Hi," he said in acknowledgment of Mrs. James's presence, then turned to Sunnie. "I thought I heard voices. What's going on?"

Sunnie took a deep breath. "Cisco, I'd like for you to meet Kody and Hunter Long's mother, Audrey James. Mrs. James, this is a new friend, Cisco Santiago. He's agreed to keep me company while we wait for the Brotherhood to find Tory."

Mrs. James turned to Cisco and smiled. "My eldest son said little about you, Mr. Santiago. I believe he has mixed feelings where you are concerned."

Just wait until Kody finds out the truth, Sunnie mused. Both he and Hunter would have a lot to come to grips with. Just as Cisco was doing right now.

Sunnie sensed his distress and knew he was uncomfortable. "Let me help you put the food away, Mrs. James. I don't want to keep Mr. James waiting out in the truck too long."

She went to work stuffing containers and covered plates in the refrigerator. Meanwhile, Cisco and Mrs. James stood in wary silence and studied each other. Sunnie couldn't stuff the food away fast enough.

Finally she was done and turned to take Mrs. James's hand. "I can't thank you enough. You were so kind to think of us." Sunnie was trying to steer the older woman toward the door.

Mrs. James slowed and turned to face Cisco eye to eye in a distinctly non-Navajo move. "Thank you for taking care of our little cousin. Sunnie means a great deal to us. We would be unhappy to learn anything bad had happened to her."

Sunnie was surprised to hear Mrs. James say such things. She hadn't thought any of her distant clansmen thought much about her welfare at all. Anxious to send Mrs. James out the door for Cisco's sake, she didn't let herself dwell on the older woman's words.

Cisco nodded to Mrs. James, but he seemed unable to speak.

"You have familiar eyes, Mr. Santiago," the older woman said all of sudden. "Do you know my younger son, Hunter? Your eyes and his are very much alike."

Cisco's demeanor changed in an instant. Sunnie felt him tense and saw that he was trying hard to school his expression.

"Nice to meet you," he told Mrs. James abruptly. "I have work to do." With that, he spun and disappeared back down the hall toward Tory's office.

Sunnie made excuses to Mrs. James, who seemed a bit startled at both Cisco's familiar appearance and his rude behavior. And in a minute or two the older woman was out the door and back in the truck, driving away with her husband.

Not able to think of what best to say to Cisco at this moment, Sunnie decided against saying anything at all. Instead she went to fix them something to eat.

Sunnie set down her fork and passed Cisco the salt. The two of them still hadn't managed more than a few words since she'd reheated one of Mrs. James's casseroles and they'd sat down to eat it.

Wanting to help and feeling his unease, Sunnie tried a little casual conversation. "How's the code breaking going?"

He shrugged and gave her a wry smile. "It would go faster if my mind didn't wander."

"Are you thinking of your father's murder?"

"That's one of the things."

She ignored the obvious question about the other things. "You know, I've been thinking about what you told me of your father. You said he worked hiding people for the U.S. Marshal's Service and that he left that job abruptly. Do you think one of the criminals might've threatened him or his family? Maybe he was scared. And then maybe that same bad guy followed him here and murdered him."

"That was one of the theories when he died. But all the investigations led nowhere."

"But suppose the criminal was protected. The information might've been classified or something."

Cisco shook his head and pushed away his half-eaten plate of food. "No one executes a lawman and gets away with it forever, *míja*. There have been several people who've reopened investigations into the murder over the years. Including, I believe, one done by an FBI agent named Kody Long.

"No," he added. "I need to talk to someone who was here on the reservation at the time and was interested in the case."

"You should talk to Kody and Hunter, then. I mean,

would you necessarily have to tell them about your relationship just to talk about the investigation?"

Cisco actually chuckled as he got up from the table.
"And just why would a complete stranger to the reservation be so interested in an old murder case? Don't you
suppose Hunter and Kody might want to know the
answer to that question before they told me anything?"

Sunnie could hear a hint of desperation coloring his
words and knew the internal indecision he felt toward
his brothers was building now that he'd met their
mother. She wanted to reach out to him, wanted to find
ways to help him settle his conflicted emotions.

But she had plenty of her own conflicts—and most
of them were now centering on the Latino bounty hunter
who'd gotten under her skin.

So when he cleared his throat and said, "Think I'll
go back to work on the code. It's the best use of my time
at the moment," she let him walk away.

Hours later, Cisco's frustration was mounting. He
almost had the notebook code busted. One more
symbol decoded here, another couple of lines deci-
phered there, and the whole freakin' code would fall
into his lap.

But every time he got right to the edge of the answers,
his mind played tricks. He would hear Sunnie in the
other parts of the cabin—in the kitchen doing dishes, in
the front room playing the radio. And mental pictures
of her edged out everything else.

Now he could hear her in the bathroom, taking a
shower, and his damned brain went off on a holiday

fling into wild imaginings. At the same time, his body rushed to pump blood to his groin.

Hell.

If only he hadn't seen her eyes in the throes of passion. Things would be a lot simpler if he'd never touched her, never tasted her. If he'd didn't know about the spot on the inside of her thigh that quivered whenever he touched it, he wouldn't still be thinking about that instead of doing the work he knew how to do.

They were not meant for anything long-term, that much was obvious. But the two of them together in the heat of savage lovemaking…now that was the kind of glorious coupling that poets had written about over the ages.

With any sense at all, however, he would keep his hands to himself. She seemed to be teetering on the brink of a breakdown over the kidnapping of her friend. Everything in her world was shifting at the moment, and he refused to be the catalyst for the earthquake he feared was imminent.

He heard her enter the room behind him, but she didn't speak. And he didn't turn. This was not a good time for him to have to look at her beautiful face. His nerves were strung tight, his body hard and ready.

She slipped up close and laid her hands on his shoulders. "How's it going? Need to take a break?"

Son of a gun. Turning her down now was going to be the hardest thing he had ever done.

Chapter 13

"Go to bed, *mija*. It looks like I'll be here most of the night."

"Go to bed *alone?*" Sunnie punched him in the bicep, hard. "You're turning me down?"

"Afraid so." Cisco could scarcely believe he was doing this.

Trying to keep his gaze locked on the computer screen and off what he knew would be a growing annoyance in her eyes, he fought to think of something to say that wouldn't give him away.

"It's been a hard day. Neither of us got much sleep last night." Well, if that wasn't lame, he didn't know what was. "Uh… Look, I promised to watch out for you. Protect you. That doesn't include jumping your bones whenever the mood strikes."

"But we already…"

"Yeah, we did. And it wasn't smart. I'm not proud of losing control like that."

She stood quietly behind him. He could feel her disappointment right through the hands that were finally loosening their grip on his shoulders.

"Then can't we wrestle? I don't think I can sleep without some exercise. Go a few rounds with me, Cisco?"

One round. One more touch. And it would be all over.

He tried to ignore the bone-weariness that seeped through his veins like a melancholy song. It was clear Sunnie was loved by nearly everyone in her world. She might not realize it at the moment because she'd been blinded by some tragedy that had colored her life. But he'd seen the truth. Every Brotherhood member he'd met so far had gazed down on her like a beloved little sister. Even Mrs. James's feelings for her seemed clear enough.

Sunnie had known love. Lots of it. He would bet that she knew what it was to be important in someone's life. To be cared for and worried over. Her parents had taught her about love. About caring for another human being.

That made her different. One hundred eighty degrees different. His own mother might've cared about him once. Maybe. But by the time he was a teen his mother's main concern had been his father's whereabouts and then later how many drugs she could buy. His father hadn't given a crap about either one of them.

How could he ever learn how to give love if he'd never been taught? For most of his life he'd had no trouble staying numb to the advances of women who wanted more from him than he could provide. And now that he'd met someone who actually made him *feel* things, it was clear this time he should stay away.

He and Sunnie might as well come from opposite sides of the emotional universe. They had no business being together for any reason at all.

"I said I was too tied up," he muttered between clenched teeth.

She said nothing for a long few seconds. "Right," she finally clipped out. "Then I'll just go and leave you to it."

A second later the door to the home office slammed, and he was once again all alone—the same as he'd been for his whole freakin' life.

Sunnie lay down fully clothed on the wide double bed in the Plant Tender's private room. Tory had once slept here amongst the plants and flowers and books. She had always loved the spicy scent of sage and the musky smells of medicine herbs drying. Sunnie breathed them in now.

Tory. A lone tear slipped from the corner of her eye. She rubbed a hand across the ache in her chest. Damn, but it hurt something awful to think of Tory with the Skinwalkers. Sunnie would gladly trade herself to them if it would mean setting her friend free.

The moment of deep sorrow blurred her vision and left a burning sensation in her stomach. The feelings brought back all the pain and anguish she'd felt six months ago. Grief, once again fresh and deadly, crept into her mind and stole her spirit.

Dammit. She'd worked so long and hard to fight off the sense of loss and guilt over her father's death. The death she couldn't have stopped but knew she had caused. She refused to give in to it again.

Tory had been the one to bring her around physically then. But she would hate knowing that Sunnie had left with a twisted will to go on and a contorted reason to survive. Revenge. The thought of taking out the Navajo Wolf, of doing to him what was done to her father, had been all the medicine she'd needed in order to set one foot in front of the other.

Tory had shared what she'd recently learned of the Navajo Way. Sunnie had known those things all her life but knew Tory had just been hoping to give her an incentive to live.

Harmony and balance are not passive concepts, Tory had told her. *They're the struggle to hold off evil. To fight against discord at every turn.*

Sunnie had taken her friend's words literally. She would not be passive. And she would proactively fight the evil in the only way she knew how: killing the Wolf.

Today her friend had been taken. And tonight Sunnie had been turned away by someone she had grown to care about. That had hurt. But over the last few days of being with Cisco something inside her had drastically changed. Some new light of knowledge was now powerfully illuminating everything in her world.

Suddenly, surprisingly, she no longer had to kill to find relief from her grief. Helping Cisco, being with him, caring about his troubles and trying to lessen his burdens had become more important than the quick shot of revenge.

But she was going to have to find some way to make

Cisco understand her reasoning. To let her be his partner in all ways. To assist in his search for the truth of what happened to his father. To help him accept his brothers and the relationships they could provide. He was a lonely man who obviously needed a family.

For a fleeting moment Sunnie wondered if that meant she was in love. Did this need to help him, to soothe his spirit and stand beside him, mean the kind of man-woman love she had heard about all her life?

It was certainly like nothing she had ever known, not even with her fiancé. And she was sure it could not last.

Frustrated with not being able to do anything for the two people she cared about the most, Sunnie closed her eyes. Maybe in an hour or two she would try getting Cisco to talk to her again. Or maybe by then he would come to bed with her.

Sighing and imagining her worries would make her toss and turn all night, Sunnie instead fell immediately into a deep, dreamless sleep.

A shaft of light slanting through the window blinds brought her completely awake. She'd actually slept all the way through the night. But what had happened to Cisco?

Making her way toward the kitchen, she smelled coffee brewing. Not sure what she would find when she stepped through the doorway, the sight that met her eyes nearly took her to her knees.

Cisco stood at the stove with his back to her. He was working there in his jeans without shoes or a shirt, and the magnificent sight of all that naked male muscle took her breath and left her heart pounding. His hair appeared to be wet from a shower, and her fingers itched with the urge to run through the damp, silky strands.

She cleared her throat and he turned. "There you are, *mija.* Coffee's ready. Can I interest you in fry bread and honey? Mrs. James left the fry bread, and I guess Tory's the one with the sweet tooth. I found a half dozen full honey jars in a cabinet."

"Coffee for sure," she managed. "Fry bread maybe."

Cisco smiled and her legs went all wobbly again. "Hey, I'm just heating the stuff up," he said with a grin. "You have any complaints about the taste, take it up with the cook."

Sunnie grabbed a mug of coffee and slid into a chair at the kitchen table. "Did you get any sleep at all?"

He set a platter with the fry bread down in front of her place and took a seat himself. "Not much. But it doesn't matter." Beaming, he fairly shimmered with a kind of tension that drove her to the edge of her seat. "I cracked the code, Sunnie. I've even managed to translate the first few pages of the notebook."

"Terrific," she said past the lump that had jumped into her throat. "Is it going to lead us to Tory?"

"I don't know for sure. Deciphering each word is slow going. But I do know which Skinwalker wrote it. The idiot scratched out his own name in symbols to help him remember the code."

Gulping a sip of the hot coffee, Sunnie tried to remain calm. "Have you notified the Brotherhood?"

"Not yet. I was waiting to discuss it with you first."

It was what she'd hoped for, dreamed about. He wanted her help in making a decision. He needed her to be a part of his life.

"Call the Brotherhood first." Her heart actually felt a little lighter. "Knowing the Skinwalker's name should be a tremendous help for locating Tory. You and I will have plenty of time to talk."

Her mind fluttered on the edge of joy. Cisco wanted her beside him and Tory was almost saved. Things were finally going in the right direction.

"It's probably Hunter or Kody Long I should call first. Michael might not even be taking calls. Right?"

She nodded, knowing how hard calling his half brothers would be. "Would you rather I do it?"

Putting his hand over hers on the table, he stopped smiling and gazed deeply into her eyes. "As much as I value your advice and opinion, I can't let you help me like that. You and I are friends, but the Longs are your family. I'll be leaving here one day soon and I won't take any chances of coming between you and your loved ones."

What? The fluttering in her chest turned to a punch in the gut. He didn't see their relationship the same way she did at all.

It was a setback. A major disappointment she could've done without. But she refused to let him leave her devastated the way she'd been before he'd arrived.

What had passed between them shouldn't have been mistaken for love in the first place. Only a woman with no parents or siblings around to give her advice would've been stupid enough to turn it into something more. He was a good guy, one of the few she'd known. He'd paid attention to the skinny girl with a chip on her shoulder. And he was sexy as hell.

Meeting a sensual good guy and having great sex was

not grounds to start building an entire imaginary relationship. What an idiot she'd been.

However, understanding that she had been foolish and sitting here with a smile on her face when she wished she could virtually disappear were two entirely different things. She pushed her chair back and stood up.

"Call Hunter. I'll go shower."

"But…"

She didn't stick around long enough to hear the rest.

Cisco had the kitchen cleared and heard Sunnie getting out of the shower at the same time someone pulled up out in front. He had called Hunter and told him he had important news.

Conflicted about having to once again face a man with his own eyes, a man who had had the father he'd always wanted and had been denied, Cisco wished there was some other way to do this.

But he knew better. Sucking up his courage and throwing on his jacket, he went out alone to greet Hunter.

The door to the white Tribal Police SUV opened as Cisco stepped off the porch. Hunter spotted him and walked over but didn't give the usual Navajo greeting.

"Where's Sunnie?" Hunter asked without any pretense of civility.

"Finishing a shower. She'll be with us in a minute."

"What's so important?"

Cisco pulled out the notebook. "Sunnie and I found this yesterday. Out in the woods, near where the Plant Tender was taken."

Hunter took the book and studied it for a moment. "It's in some kind of code?"

Cisco nodded his head. "Yeah, but I broke the code last night and translated a few of the pages."

"*You* broke the code?"

The flash of anger surged, but Cisco fought to keep it under control. "It's one of the things I've taught myself to do. Sunnie and I knew Michael Ayze would be too busy, so I gave it a shot. And I came up with something."

Cisco heard the door opening behind his back and felt Sunnie step to his side. "The man who owns that notebook refers to himself as the Burrowing Owl. I'm assuming that's some kind of Skinwalker."

Hunter shot a glance over at Sunnie and then narrowed his eyes back on Cisco. "Finding a Skinwalker notebook in a code that only you can decipher is pretty convenient." He hesitated, scowled and finally said, "You never told us what you were doing on the reservation. Why should I believe you? And how should I know you're not working with the Skinwalkers against us?"

Sunnie pulled on Cisco's arm to get his attention. "Tell him," she urged.

"Yeah, tell me," Hunter repeated.

Dammit. No choice now but just to say it. "I came to dig into a murder that happened here on the reservation a long time ago. The killing of a man named Sam Long."

He could see Hunter's shock, though the other man hid it fairly well. If Cisco hadn't trained himself to see beyond the normal, he would've missed the look entirely.

"My father," Hunter said through gritted teeth. "Why?"

This was it, the time for words he had dreaded. "Because he was my father, too."

Now the looks in those familiar eyes of Hunter's were ones Cisco recognized all too well. Disbelief. Then a moment of realization. Then hurt. Anger.

"My mother said she thought your eyes looked like mine. I hadn't noticed before, but now…" Hunter's words failed him for a second, but he recovered quickly. "How old are you? And how long have you known?"

"I'm thirty-three."

"About the same as me." Hunter's expression changed over to comprehension, but anger still simmered underneath.

Cisco quickly added, "And I only figured out who my father was after my mother died last year. I had never even known his last name."

"Then your mother and my father weren't married?"

Cisco shook his head. That was a bone that had been sticking in his throat for all of his life.

"So the bastard had bastard children." Hunter spit the words like a curse. "It figures. I wonder how many more there might be out there."

Cisco fisted his hands, but Sunnie grabbed his elbow.

"You and your father didn't get along well?" Sunnie asked Hunter.

"I was overjoyed when he died. It was finally the end of my mother's pain. If I'd been a little older, I would've killed him myself the next time he laid a hand on her."

"Did Kody feel the same as you?" Sunnie asked.

Hunter looked taken back. "Damn. I've forgotten about my brother. This is going to be a real shock to him.

Just a moment. I'd better call him." He pulled out his phone and spoke to Kody, but all he said was that he had something important to say in person.

"Kody will be here in a while," he said as he hung up. "My brother never knew about our father's abuse of our mother. She would never allow me to tell anyone. Not even Kody. He'd been sent away to boarding school in the Navajo traditional way, while I stayed home to help out. For years he blamed himself for our father's death, thinking if he'd been here that he could've stopped the murder. But I believe that would've been impossible."

Suddenly Cisco began putting things together. And he had a feeling that Hunter had been doing some thinking along the same lines.

"Have you ever wondered if it's possible the body they recovered wasn't his?"

Hunter looked surprised, but only for a split second. "It's been in the back of my mind for a long time, yeah. But I can't quite figure out why my father would fake his own death. What he could've hoped to gain?"

"Can't you?" Cisco was shocked by his own words, but instinct told him his half brother's mind was squarely in the same place as his. "You're sure you haven't wondered about the coincidental timing of your father's death and the appearance of the Navajo Wolf?"

Hunter scowled. "Holy crap. Now that you mention it, I've had dreams of the Navajo Wolf with my father's face. But I thought it was just my old anger coming back when I was asleep and couldn't control it.

"Several years ago Lucas Tso told me he had also

seen my father as the Wolf in his dreams," Hunter added. "We thought it was weird for both of us to see the same thing, but we let it slide."

"Then it's possible?"

Hunter nodded.

"Wait," Sunnie broke in. "You two are saying you believe your own father faked his death in order to become the Navajo Wolf? Are you serious?"

"I wish I wasn't," Cisco muttered. "'Cause if I was joking, then I wouldn't be feeling so guilty about old Shorty Tom's death."

Hunter blinked, then set his jaw. "Shorty was there in the canyon that day. The first one to find the body. You think the Skinwalkers killed him because you were going to question him about the murder?" Hunter shut his mouth, then opened it again with a snarl. "Son of a gun. That's one more reason to believe we're guessing right about our father being the Navajo Wolf."

Our father. It took Cisco a minute to process the meaning of those words. He had never been a part of an *our* before. *We* and *us* were going to be every bit as foreign sounding. He would need time to absorb all the new emotions in suddenly finding himself a member of a family.

"Look…" He tried to explain his sense of urgency. "This stuff between us may take a while to sort out, but Tory Wauneka doesn't have time to wait. Even knowing our father is the Navajo Wolf doesn't help us find her.

"I think the Brotherhood should work first on any information that might lead to her," Cisco added. "The name I found in that notebook was Professor Richard Yellowhorse. Ring any bells?"

"You bet it does," Hunter said with a groan. "He's supposedly Michael Ayze's friend and associate at the Dine College. But I never have trusted that sneaky bastard. It fits he would write a journal in his own code. Guy thinks he's a genius and better at symbolism even than Michael.

"So he's the Skinwalker Owl, huh?" Hunter narrowed his eyes in thought. "There's one or two members of the Brotherhood who'll have good reason to find that a very interesting and useful piece of information."

The sound of a truck pulling up the grade reached their ears. Hunter turned his head, listened, then swung back to Cisco and Sunnie.

"That's my brother's truck approaching. Listen, I agree that we need to concentrate our efforts on rescuing the Plant Tender before anything else. And there's a lot of new information for Kody to accept. I'm going to suggest you let me tell him about our being half brothers in my own time. I may even decide to tell my mother first and have her help me explain. She'll have a right to know, too. And she's been the one who has always tried to keep Kody in the dark about his father."

"Okay." Cisco nodded. "I agree you know your brother best. But I'd just as soon Kody didn't think I was too much a coward to tell him the truth."

Hunter grinned. "No, Brother. Trust me on this one. I won't let him think that."

Kody climbed down from his truck and joined them. Cisco decided to let Hunter take the lead and do most of the talking. Hunter explained to his brother about the notebook and the Skinwalker Owl but never mentioned anything about their relationship to Cisco.

At last Hunter said to Kody, "Cisco and I are working on a theory about the Navajo Wolf. But we think it would be wise to rescue the Plant Tender before making any more moves in that direction. You agree?"

Kody was a lawman, too, accustomed to listening for hidden meanings. Cisco could see the wheels turning as he studied him and Hunter. Did Kody notice the resemblance? If he did, he must've decided finding Tory was the more important consideration at the moment.

He nodded, accepting everything Hunter told him without question. At least without questioning it aloud.

The two Long brothers made a plan for notifying the Brotherhood about the notebook and for capturing the traitor Yellowhorse. Cisco stood quietly with his arm around Sunnie and waited to see what would happen next.

Before they left, Hunter stopped and handed Cisco back the notebook. "I doubt if Michael will have time to do anything with this for a while. But it might contain more information about the Skinwalkers—or the Wolf. Keep working on decoding it, will you?"

Cisco gave a sharp nod in reply. "And you go find the Plant Tender."

Sunnie took Hunter's hand. "Yes, save Tory, cousin. And soon. I can't stand thinking of her with them."

The afternoon wore thin for Sunnie and Cisco. She paced the Plant Tender's cabin, unable to sit as she desperately tried to stem her terror and control her worsening unease about Tory. But nothing was working.

Cisco was back at the computer, working on the coded notebook. She knew he was still having trouble with it and felt the problems had more to do with his thinking of his father and half brothers than with the translations.

He needed a break. And she would love to help him out with that. The poor guy had been at it for nearly twenty-four hours now. But last night he'd refused to let go. She wondered how to make today any different.

The light from outside became muted, throwing the cabin into shadows. Sunnie could smell the ozone in the air and sensed the inside plants perking up and raising their faces for moisture. Deciding that one thing she could do to help her friend would be to water her plants, Sunnie went in search of a watering can.

But the minute the can was in her hand Sunnie could feel Tory's presence. Her scent was strong, and Sunnie's stomach began to churn with worry again.

She watered a few plants, then wandered into the office and pulled up a chair beside Cisco, who was dressed in comfy jeans and T-shirt. "How's it going?"

"Still slow."

"Can I see?" She slapped a hand on his arm and peeked over his shoulder, reading the pages he had already decoded.

"That's not a good idea. I've…" He tried to conceal his work, but she stood and twisted and caught the words.

"Does that say what I think it says?" A horrible tightness clutched at her throat and squeezed her chest. "The

Skinwalkers are planning on killing Tory? But…why? If Michael does what they ask, why would they do that?"

Cisco shook his head. "The best I can make out, this Owl guy doesn't want any witnesses left. Plus, I think he's eager to cause the Brotherhood casualties. I get the feeling he particularly wants to hurt Michael Ayze."

She shifted away from Cisco and walked to the window. Outside, a soft female rain had begun to fall. Drops gently touched the windowpane and streamed downward, blurring the view. The view from her eyes had also began to blur as sheer despair left her empty and vulnerable. Her shoulders slumped and wetness leaked steadily down her cheeks.

"Hey, cut that out." Cisco pushed back his chair and came up beside her. "You're feeling sorry for yourself, and I won't have it."

He roughly grabbed her by the shoulders and spun her around. She lowered her eyes to avoid his glare and wrapped her arms around her waist.

"I am not," she moaned, wishing her voice didn't sound so full of pain. "I'm not feeling sorry for myself. I'm… I'm…" She didn't know what she was except for frightened half out of her wits over her friend's life.

Lifting her chin with his fingers, Cisco forced her to look at him. "You're tougher than this, dammit. I liked you better before, when you were raging against the injustice. When you were angry.

"I just don't know how to deal with you like this." His voice cracked, as though his throat had filled with dust. "How about if you hit me? Give it your best shot."

At the sound of his concern, her eyes brimmed over,

and she had to lean her forehead against his chest in order to continue standing.

"Aw, hell." He folded her into his arms and swore softly under his breath.

Her own voice hitched on one last sob as she said, "I hate them. And I'm petrified enough for Tory that I can't think." She gulped a breath, slowed down. "I'm just so angry and frustrated."

Swinging her up in his arms, he cradled her against him like a baby. He took two slow steps away from the window, then picked up speed as he carried her down the hallway.

Chapter 14

Cisco eased down on the bed with Sunnie still in his arms. She sat immobile and silent in his lap. The sobbing had stopped, but tears continued to leak from her eyes. It was all too quiet and too docile for the woman he'd grown to know.

Brushing the hair back from her face, he began crooning a Mexican lullaby. A song he hadn't thought of in years. He rocked her, singing and stroking her hair.

In a little while, she shifted and knuckled back the last of the tears. "Thank you, Cisco."

He gazed down at the top of her head and that glorious ebony hair. "Thank me for what? I haven't done anything."

She snuggled in closer. "You've done more than you'll probably ever know." Her breath was warm against his neck and a thrill went up his spine. "But thanks just for being here. I'm not sure what I would've done without you."

Bending, he kissed her cheek, then ran tiny kisses down the velvet skin of her neck. "You're welcome," he whispered. "But you would've done fine without me. You're tough, sugar. Beautiful and tough."

His heart began pounding as he could swear he actually felt the tension and energy growing inside her. It made him wonder how much more he could do to jangle her nerves. To take her mind off her friend.

Lifting her hand, he turned it palm up and gently placed his mouth just there in the middle. A soft little gasp escaped her lips as he ran his tongue over the tender, pale skin.

"I…" Her voice jolted as he blew a breath over the moisture he'd created with his kiss. "I'm not so tough. Right now I'm feeling pretty weak."

"Yeah?" He hadn't let go of her hand and now laid it over his heart. "You could've fooled me. Your pulse is racing like you're ready to fight. It matches my heartbeat. Feel it?"

"Uh-huh." Her body trembled in his arms. "What are you doing?"

"Seducing you gently. You mind?"

"But I thought you said…"

He brushed his lips over her mouth to shut her up. "I want to know what happens between us without the flash, *mija.* We've been all fire and thunderstorms together so far, but this time I want embers and mist first."

"Then kiss me." She lifted her head and strained to reach his lips.

"Not yet." He captured her arms so she couldn't wriggle away, then bent again to lick his way down her throat in drugging little circles.

Rain splashed quietly against the window and left the room in soft afternoon shadows. With another slide of his tongue over her silky skin and another brush of her satin hair over his bare arms, Cisco felt the heat building, threatening to put a torch to his good intentions. But he doused the flame. For the moment.

When Sunnie's limbs finally went weak and she quit stirring and relaxed, he laid her back on the bed and covered her body with his own. It was then that he kissed her lips.

But still he held off. He wanted to send them both over easy, with clever touches and gentle, smooth, ever-so-slow kisses. Deepening this kiss a little at a time, though, he found himself getting caught in his own trap. Desperation to take her fast instead of slow started as a niggle in his groin and grew to an impossible demand within seconds.

He groaned out her name, heard her echo his in return. That's when he felt her surrender. A subtle change at first, her body began yielding to his in a whole new way. It was erotic. He had to grit his teeth against the blood pulsing in his veins. But before going too far, he snatched back his control.

"Let me take you away for once, *mi amor*," he said on a breath. "Forget everything but this. Us. Right now."

Raising up on an elbow, he gazed down at her sensuous, languid body. She blinked and looked up at him from heavy-lidded and lust-filled eyes.

"I want to know what gives you pleasure," he murmured as he began to undress her. "Does my mouth here on the curve of your neck make you moan or sigh?"

She sighed.

He pulled off her jeans and quickly disposed of his own clothes. "How about here on the inside of your thigh," he said as he placed a gentle kiss where he'd indicated.

She moaned in response and he felt her body quiver.

"Trust me, Sunnie. Let me." He gazed at her face.

The tenderness in her eyes nearly took away his resolve. No one had ever looked at him with that expression. Never in his memory.

Not sure he could manage to hold off if he had to continue like this, he rolled her over on her stomach. He stroked the muscles of her back, admiring the smoothness and the strength under his fingers. Moving his hands lower, he used his touch and his tongue to run along the ridge of her spine.

For long minutes he patiently teased and fondled and licked, smiling when she fisted her hands in the sheets and groaned helplessly. He brought her up once, heard the panting sounds she was making, then backed off. But when the rain stopped, Cisco knew it was time to meet the call. To earn her complete trust.

Rolling her again, he advanced his demands and she responded instantly. He filled her slowly, not ready to rush now that they both teetered on the edge. She squirmed when he stopped inside her, and his brain went giddy with delight in her.

"Easy now," he murmured. "Not yet. I want *everything* this time."

He threaded his fingers in her rich, silky hair and took her breast into his mouth, sucking until he heard her mewling noises become more high-pitched. The two of them were on the brink of something special. Something so wonderful he couldn't manage to come up with a name for it.

When she arched her hips against him, he lifted his head and stared down at the liquid black eyes swimming with urgency and…that same something wonderful.

"Take everything, then, Cisco," she murmured through a gasp. "Take it all. I'll give you whatever you want—always."

The fire combusted, kindled and flared, surprisingly fast for such a slow burn. It took them both over in a spectacular shower of flaming sparks.

Sunnie floated on a cottony cloud of ecstasy. Her body felt disengaged from her spirit. Somewhere in the back of her mind she struggled to find her footing. But the pleasurable tingles still resonating from deep inside made thinking impossible. So she eased up on herself and let the cloud carry her off on currents of what had to be love.

Drifting to sleep, she suddenly found herself running out of the clouds and into the darkness. Running away from something? No, running down a path toward the light. There was something she needed to remember, something so important she knew it would mean life or death.

In an instant, a horrific snake, at least twelve feet high standing on its tail, appeared in the path. She battled it back with her fists until a gun appeared in her hand. She shot the snake, crawled over the corpse and kept running.

Tiring, she gulped in air but continued moving toward the light. Then she heard it. The cry in the distance. More a weeping than a wailing.

Sunnie fought to find her way. The path narrowed, became more difficult to navigate. Where was the light now? Where was the person who'd cried? She knew the time grew shorter. If she was going to find and help someone, it would have to be now.

Panicked, she began to call out. But the sound of her voice only echoed off unseen hills. Her calls turned to screams. Her voice grew taut and louder. Tears blinded her until she had to stop and swipe away the blurry wetness. Hysteria, quick, cold, deadly, at last took her over.

"Sunnie, wake up now," Cisco's voice intruded on the darkness. "I'm right here. You're okay. You're having a nightmare."

Opening her eyes, she looked up into the concerned gaze of a man who wanted to help. The man who had suddenly become like a drink of water in a dry desert where she had long been thirsting.

She wrapped her arms around his neck and held on, waiting for the dizzying effects of the dream to wear off.

When she could breathe easier, she fought to find her voice. "We have to do something to help Tory," she said with a groan. "I can't sit here, safe and warm and happy, while the Skinwalkers kill her. I can't."

"What can we do, *míja?* The Brotherhood is looking."

"We have to try to find her. We must. I must."

Cisco shook his head and leaned back to look at her.

"Do you have any new ideas? 'Cause if you don't, we can't just go…"

"Maybe I can remember how to get to the Navajo Wolf's hideout. It's been years since I was there. But if I really try, if you help me, maybe together we can locate the place."

"Sounds like a long shot. And even if you manage to find it, that doesn't necessarily mean Tory is being kept there."

"I think she is. The dream…"

Sunnie stopped herself and stared up into his eyes, letting her own eyes plead with him. "Help me. Come with me. Don't force me to stay here doing nothing while Tory is dying. It will kill me for sure this time."

He eased her against his chest and enfolded her in his arms. "What do you mean by 'this time'?"

She couldn't face the truth yet. Sunnie had avoided talking about the horror to anyone and had even managed to sometimes forget about it. But she'd known the time for speaking the words aloud would someday come. And someday drew closer.

Cisco was the last person she wanted to shock by telling him of her actions—her inactions. But he would end up being the one, she felt sure of it in her heart.

Just not now. Another little while of keeping him as a friend, a lover. That's all she asked. Just a few more hours of pretending everything would work out in the end.

Sunnie was well aware Cisco hadn't been thrilled at the idea of driving them around outside. Especially not this close to sunset, and in the Plant Tender's SUV, which he'd never driven before. But at least the rain had stopped for now.

"You believe the place was on a cliff overlooking the San Juan River?" he asked her. "Why don't you try visualizing the route in your head. Close your eyes and…"

"Quit the New Age stuff," she mumbled irritably. "It's not like I haven't been trying. I've tried for months."

The annoyance and frustration were clear in her voice, though she'd thought to hide them. Tilting her head, she stared over at the last of the ponderosa forests on the high plateau and then glanced out the windshield toward the peach-colored sandstone ramparts straight ahead.

Glad the rain had stopped for now, she looked at her homeland through the glass and hoped it wouldn't snow again. But as it was the season when thunder and snakes sleep, she was surprised at seeing so much color and life in Dinetah.

They drove past a hogan surrounded with green piñon and golden grasses. Outside, under a basketball hoop, youngsters dressed in lipstick-red jackets used the opportunity to take a few shots while the rain slacked off. One of them bounced the ball on the wet granite below the hoop.

An old grandmother who looked as though she'd shriveled from the rain stood on the porch nearby with a baby in her arms. Sunnie's stomach gave a quick jitter at the sight of the infant, and she wondered what it would feel like to hold such a tiny one. Her mind wandered off to thoughts of diapers and bottles and cute pink outfits with tiny feet sewn right in.

She snuck a glance at Cisco's profile and wondered

if he'd ever thought of having children. Well, as more than just a mistake of not being prepared, that is.

Silly idea, she thought glumly as she turned to look away from the dangerous bounty hunter dressed in a black leather jacket. It was just plain stupid to think of him in any way that might include a future. He wasn't a tomorrow kind of guy.

"There," she shouted as she pointed. "Turn right there."

"Hell," Cisco muttered as he swung the wheel and felt the tires slide against the pavement. "Next time give me a few seconds' notice, will you?"

"Sorry, but things are finally starting to look more familiar."

Cisco scanned the scenery just as the moody dove-gray skies gave way to a hint of waning sunlight. Then a rainbow suddenly appeared over towering buttes to the north, and the sight gave him a jolt.

"Look," he said as he gestured toward the pastel-striped sky. "That's the direction where we're headed. You think it's a sign that we're on the right track?"

"How very fanciful of you, Bounty Hunter." She gazed out the windshield, then turned her head and rolled her eyes. "I didn't know you had an artistic streak."

"I don't." But he did appreciate a beautiful picture and had a couple of rooms full of expensive artwork to prove it.

Shooting a glance in her direction, he compared her rare beauty to all the art and natural wonders he had ever beheld. None of them even came close.

He would gladly give up every one of his paintings,

the houses and all the bank accounts he possessed if they could find Tory alive and well. The idea that this search might be a fruitless waste of time kept nagging at him. He didn't really understand what losing a friend would do to Sunnie. But he knew what seeing her devastated and heartbroken would do to him.

Sunnie twisted her hands as they lay in her lap. "I think we turned left from here."

"You think?"

"I was only there once and I wasn't driving. Everything about that trip is fuzzy. The land is all starting to look the same."

The minute she'd said the words, the sky grew wild with raspberry and plum streaks from the setting sun. A reddish glow cast everything in strange and eerie fire streaks. It was different and disorienting.

"Now nothing looks the same," she said with a hitch in her voice. "What are we going to do, Cisco? We'll never find it in time."

"Take it easy. I've often read of the 'enduring Navajo' and thought you people were supposed to be good at patience and waiting." His own voice was becoming hoarse with concern and frustration. "Have I ever told you about tracking down Slick Mancusco, the art forger?"

"No. But the sun has dropped below a cliff now and things seem familiar again. Turn left up ahead, beside that house with the green roof and the Russian olive trees."

He guided the SUV toward distant mesas as the last of the sun's rays disappearing behind the mountains turned the environment to dusky blue. "You want to hear about how I couldn't follow old Slick by tracing his money so instead had to start buying up his forgeries until he came to me? That took months of steady endurance."

"You bought forged paintings? Had you ever bought good art before?"

"Some." He flipped on the headlights and slowed down.

"But how did you know what was real and what wasn't?"

"I was an Art History major in college. Eventually took several classes on the old masters and various oil techniques in Florence."

"Oh." Sunnie seemed lost for a moment, but he could sense her mind at work. He could only hope he'd taken her focus off her friend for a little while.

"What'd you do with the art you bought from him?"

"I kept some of it. A few of the better pieces."

"Are they hanging in your home? Uh—where is it that you actually live, anyway?"

How had the conversation turned to home? He had houses, lots of them. But he'd never lived in a real home. That was one of the many things they didn't share in common.

He dragged in a breath. "I own several places. Most of them have big, cold rooms with books, paintings and sculpture. Can't say I spend much time in any of them."

She made a face as if she didn't care for the picture he'd drawn. He should have known she would feel that way. With all her clan and family, any place she went would soon feel full of life, warm and safe.

He had no life. What could he offer her? Nothing but cold, empty rooms, endless vacant nights and sterile holidays. She needed the heat and color that came from being near the people who loved you most.

Out of the darkness several white-tailed does appeared and gracefully bounded across the road in front of him. He stepped on the brakes and slowed, stopping until the last of them had disappeared again into the thick brush on the other side.

He took a deep breath and smelled wet sage and animal musk. Just then the cell phone in his pocket rang.

Answering, Cisco was surprised to hear a low, sensual female voice on the other end of the line.

"Mr. Santiago," she began hesitantly. "You don't know me. I'm Michael's wife, Alexis Ayze. I got your phone number from Hunter Long. I…um…well, I have a message for Sunnie if she's with you."

"What kind of message?"

"You're going to think this is crazy, but…" Her voice halted again as if she didn't dare tell the truth.

At this point, he wouldn't think anything she said was crazy. Or maybe it was more that everything that had happened so far had been nuts anyway. So whatever she said would sound tame.

"Go ahead," he said wryly.

"The Brotherhood knows me as the Message Bearer. I receive messages from the ancestors and take them to those who will find them useful."

"Messages. Like dreams? Or ghost sightings? And you have a message for Sunnie from one of these *ancestors?*"

At the mention of her name, Sunnie turned her head

with questions swimming in her eyes. That wasn't all he spotted in those deep, liquid browns. Fear lay buried in there, as well.

The fright was what moved him. He'd wanted to save her from it but saw now that he could do nothing to help. Perhaps this woman on the phone would say something to quiet Sunnie's fears. Even if it wasn't logical or true, a word of encouragement from a friend couldn't hurt.

"Hold on," he told Alexis and handed the phone to the beautiful woman who sat tensely beside him.

Sunnie put the cell phone to her ear and held her breath, hoping this call wouldn't be the worst news.

"Sunnie, this is Lexie Ayze. I've just had a visit from the Old Plant Tender, Shirley Nez."

"You can't have. The Old Plant Tender died several years ago."

Sunnie listened to patient silence coming over the earpiece and decided to keep her mouth shut for the time being. Lexie Ayze was one of the most down-to-earth people she'd ever met. Questioning her didn't seem smart.

"You must have heard that I am the Message Bearer," Lexie finally said. "Over the last year I've been receiving warnings and special assistance meant for the Brotherhood from their Navajo ancestors. A little while ago the Old Plant Tender came to me with a message for you."

"What could she possibly need to tell me? I'm not in the Brotherhood. I can't…"

"Shirley Nez wants you to save the New Plant Tender, Little Sister."

Sunnie remembered that Shirley had given her the name "little sister" when she'd been a teenager. No one else was still alive who would know about that. Suddenly everything Lexie Ayze had to say became extremely urgent.

"The Old Plant Tender has given me the directions to take you to the New Plant Tender," Lexie went on. "And she has sent a personal message meant to make the difference in Tory's life or death."

Sunnie panicked. "Why don't you give these directions to the Brotherhood? Or to the Bird People? They can do more to save Tory than I ever could."

"It's not my decision or choice," Lexie told her. "If you wish to share the instructions with the Brotherhood or anyone else, then it's up to you."

Great. Just what she needed. Another responsibility. Another dire choice to make.

"What's the message?" Sunnie asked but wasn't sure she really wanted the answer.

"Shirley Nez said to tell you, 'When the time comes, you will hear the cock crow three times. Take up your arms. Ignore your reservations but trust in your heart.'"

"That's it? That's the life-or-death message?"

"Word for word. Now I'll give you the driving directions. The Wolf's mansion's hidden from view by Skinwalker magic, but Shirley said you are on the right track. The New Plant Tender is at the Wolf's mansion."

As Lexie told her the various turns to reach the Skinwalker's hideout, Sunnie relayed them to Cisco. She figured that between the two of them they should be able to memorize it all. Most of the directions were fairly simple, like a turn at the large, lone tamarisk tree and another before the bridge over Salt Creek Wash.

When Lexie completed forwarding the instructions, she had one more thing to say. "Be careful, Sunnie. I want Tory saved as much as anyone, but there's something the Old Plant Tender wasn't saying. Not with words, anyway. I have the feeling the New Plant Tender's rescue may be more than what it seems. It was almost as if Shirley Nez knew Tory's kidnapping would be the start of something bigger.

"Or…maybe Shirley was trying to say this rescue would be an ending. Just don't let it be the end of you."

After Sunnie thanked Lexie and hung up, she turned to Cisco. "Tell me what to do. The Old Plant Tender insisted the message was for me. She must've had some good reason. But the Brotherhood should know about this, too, right? I mean, we can't rescue Tory all by ourselves."

"It's possible. But I agree it doesn't sound likely." Cisco didn't like her turning to him for the responsibility of making such a huge decision. "Why don't we follow the directions first and see where they lead? If they really end up at the Wolf's mansion, then we can call in reinforcements. Let's not bother the Brotherhood until we're sure."

He could see Sunnie nodding thoughtfully in the dregs of twilight. It was going to be slow going, picking their way over gravel roads and around sandstone pinnacles at night. She was bound to dwell on all the wrong possibilities if they didn't carry on a conversation while they traveled. He needed another distraction.

"If it turns out not telling the Brotherhood first was the wrong move, I hope I die along with Tory." Sunnie had opened up a whole new topic herself. One that stunned him and nearly took away his breath.

"You don't mean that," he whispered after a gulp of air.

"After last time, I swore to give my life before another loved one could be taken at my expense. I mean every word."

"That's the second time you've referred to the 'last time.' Can you tell me what happened then?"

She looked down at her hands, barely visible in the darkness. "It was six months ago. I'd been hiding from the Skinwalkers for over a year. We all knew they would never give up searching for me. But I couldn't stand the idea of moving off the reservation entirely. Not while my…father was still alive."

Cisco didn't say anything. Just waited quietly for her to continue.

"The Skinwalkers tricked me. I'd thought I was so smart and knew everything about them. I didn't know they had someone who could change voices and sound like others. One day my father got a call from me—supposedly. He was told to meet me at a trading post in the mountains. He came without question.

"In the meantime, I got a call, too. From someone who sounded like my father in trouble. I ran out of the house, never taking a moment to contact the Brotherhood."

She stopped speaking as he heard a bubble of hesitation welling up in her throat. He'd wanted her talking, but this…not about this.

"Sunnie…"

"No," she interrupted with a half sob. "I have to tell you. I must say it out loud.

"I reached him too late. I'd had enough presence of mind to sense trouble even though I hadn't called for help. So when I saw his car parked there, I crept up to the abandoned trading post on foot. I heard…"

She covered her face with her hands but kept talking. "I heard the most horrible sounds. Not the screams or cries of pain and suffering from my father. But noises more like the ripping and tearing of flesh and skin, primitive and greedy. The growling sounds of wild animals after a kill.

"I wanted to run to him and I wanted to run away. Instead I froze in terror at the sight of all that blood. They hurt me, too. But I didn't die. I didn't."

"Stop it," he said more sharply than he'd meant. "Stop seeing that in your mind. Come back to the present. It's not the same. It won't happen again."

"How can you say that?" She sobbed softly. "How can you be sure?"

"Because this time you have a secret weapon. This time you have me."

Chapter 15

Within a mile of the cliff where the Navajo Wolf's mansion was supposed to be Cisco pulled over onto the gravel shoulder and turned off the SUV.

"You couldn't have saved your father. Not even if you had thought to call the Brotherhood. There was no way any of you could've known the truth."

He shut off the interior overhead light and opened the driver's door. "But this time we'll be smarter together. I'm going to call the Brotherhood now, give them the directions. Then I'm heading over the mesa on foot to check it out."

Sunnie unbuckled and jumped out as he did. She set her jaw and stepped closer to him, waiting while he called Hunter. Only able to hear his side of the conversation, she still knew when they talked about her. Knew when Cisco promised his half brother that he would keep her safe.

As Cisco hung up, he turned to her. She saw his face clearly through the crisp night air and by the light of the stars. His expression was one she would never forget.

Without a word, he reached out and yanked her to him. He said more with the smoldering, drugging touch of lips and tongues than he could've ever said aloud.

But when he released her, he spoke with such fervor she lost her way. "Stay here, *mi vida.* Stay and be safe locked inside the SUV. I'll find out if this is the place. And if Tory is inside, I *will* bring her out to you."

Mi vida. He'd called her his life. Her heart skipped and twirled in her chest. Oh, if only she could believe in those words. But she knew better. His life was elsewhere. He was educated and rich, adventurous and exciting. And she was none of those things.

Speechless, she watched him head off over the rocks and sand, into the desert and toward who knew what danger.

Cisco crept away from Sunnie, cursing himself under his breath. When he'd looked down and seen her eyes swimming with tears, he'd been damned forever.

He was an idiot to love her. But love her he did. And with a more hopeless and yet intense emotion than he had ever felt in his life. He knew there would never be another who would touch him, his heart and his spirit, the way Sunnie had.

But there was only one thing in the world he could

give her—her friend Tory alive and well. And when he had done that, it would be time for him to leave.

He was fairly certain he'd discovered everything there was to find out here in Dinetah. And more. He'd met his half brothers. His father's death was no longer a mystery. At least not to him.

So did he have to actually come face-to-face with the man one last time to prove something? Not for any reason he could find. There were no more mysteries to solve. His mother's greatest wish was fulfilled.

As he crept across the desert toward the big house on the hill, that last thought dredged up something from deep within his gut. The knowledge that the one who had fathered him, the one his mother had unfortunately loved, that man was long gone and done. The pure evil who stood now in his place meant nothing to anyone anymore.

But for Sunnie's sake?

Sighing softly in the night, Cisco decided that there was one more thing he could give her before they parted forever. He could do what she had tried and failed.

And so he made a resolution. As he rescued Tory, he would spend a moment or two more in his bastard father's house. Just long enough to end the life that had caused such havoc and wreaked such terror amongst Sunnie's clansmen and friends.

Just long enough to kill the Navajo Wolf.

Sunnie stood for way too long looking out toward the darkness where Cisco had disappeared. She didn't know how to feel or what to be. Should she just give in to the love that was quickly consuming every cell in her body and run and hide as he'd asked? Should she begin fortifying herself for the coming pain of losing him too soon?

Or should she damn well put aside the emotions altogether and remember who and what she was? Loving Cisco had changed her world. Instead of the black pit of self-pity and hatred she had been wallowing in for the last six months, everything around her had suddenly come alive with color and light.

Deep inside, she was still the same strong, tough-willed woman she had always been. But she no longer needed revenge to restore her spirit and dissolve the guilt. The Navajo Wolf would meet his end by some other's hand or by his own greed. It didn't matter to her anymore.

The only things that mattered were saving Tory and making sure nothing happened to Cisco. He would *not* be killed or injured while rescuing her friend. She swore it.

Digging in her pocket for her phone, Sunnie stopped when she heard a car's engine in the distance. It seemed to be coming closer to her position. She hid behind a sandstone boulder and watched as another SUV with its lights off pulled up behind Tory's vehicle.

Sunnie held her breath until she could see that the SUV was a white Navajo Tribal Police unit. How had Hunter gotten here so quickly?

But it wasn't Hunter who eased out of the driver's seat and stood quietly next to the SUV. It was Lucas Tso's bride, Teal, the new Navajo Tribal policewoman. Sunnie whispered the other woman's name and came out of hiding.

"*Ya'at'eeh,*" Teal said in her own stage whisper when she spotted Sunnie. "I hoped I would find you."

"What are you doing out here? How did you know where to look for me?"

"My husband has been tracking Professor Richard Yellowhorse for the last few hours," Teal told her. "I have been right behind him. Tracking my husband, you could say." She grinned wryly through the starlight. "Lucas knows I'm here, though he doesn't much care for the idea."

"So Lucas is on his way into the Navajo Wolf's mansion, following the professor? This is really the right place, then?"

"Oh, yes. When Hunter got Cisco's call with the directions, Lucas was nearly right on top of the house. I think that damned Professor Yellowhorse-slash-Skinwalker Owl must've been only fifteen minutes ahead of you."

"So Lucas knows we're here?"

"He knows. He's stationed himself nearby, holding off and waiting for the rest of the Brotherhood and the Bird People to arrive."

"I'd better warn Cisco. I wouldn't want the two of them to kill each other by mistake." She pulled out her cell and hit the buttons for his phone.

"Don't worry about Lucas," Teal said as they waited for Cisco to answer. "My husband would never kill anyone except the Skinwalker Owl. And he'll easily sense the difference."

Cisco quietly answered his phone and Sunnie told him to watch out for Lucas. It only took a matter of a few words to get the message across. But when Sunnie hung up, she felt devastated and more alone than she'd ever been.

"It's hard, isn't it?" Teal asked softly from beside her.

"What is?"

"Being in love and watching the one you care about the most walking into danger."

"I'm not in lo—" She stopped. Lying to even herself was useless at this point. "Yeah, it is terrible, actually. It's a lot easier to take the risk yourself rather than waiting behind."

"Tell me about it. I'm not very good at the wringing-my-hands and weeping-into-a-hanky gigs. Frankly I'm a lot better with a weapon."

"Are you going inside the mansion after the Brotherhood gets here?" Sunnie suddenly realized she was definitely not one to stand silently in the background, either. She hadn't spent all that time on a rifle range for nothing.

"I'm not a medicine man and can't say the chants that will control the Skinwalker danger," Teal began. "But, by God, I can shoot better than any of them. And at the base of all that evil are human men who can be killed with a bullet just as well as with a chant. I'll be there."

Sunnie made up her mind in a heartbeat. "Hey, you cops carry other weapons in your units, don't you?"

It was long after midnight and pitch-dark when Cisco spotted Lucas's silhouette in a clump of junipers near the mansion. Though once Cisco would've said all Navajos looked alike, the truth was, each one he'd come in contact with had made a distinctive impression on him. Impressions he was sure to carry to his grave.

The two men motioned to each other and met a

little farther from the mansion, concealed by a stand of cottonwoods.

"What have you found out?" he asked Lucas in a low voice.

"Something feels all wrong about this place."

"What do you mean by *wrong?*"

Lucas hesitated, then whispered, "There's an air of expectant death here." He reached down and actually touched a prairie dog that leaned half out of its hole, still as a statue. "It's as though the very ground is dying." The prairie dog never stirred.

The unnatural sight put a knife of fear into Cisco's gut. "Do you think that means they're going to kill Tory at any minute instead of waiting?"

"No. I can feel the Plant Tender's lifeblood still beating strong and true. I sense no imminent danger there. This is something else. Something far more sinister."

Cisco didn't like any of it. The night suffocated him and the ground beneath his feet pulled him down. "I want to get Tory out of that place now. Now that we've broken through the magic and can see the mansion, have you found out where they're holding her? Do they also have a security system on the house?"

"There were vultures stationed outside when I arrived. But our Bird People allies have arrived and quietly disposed of them. I've seen nothing else." Lucas shifted in the dark. "As to where they're holding the Plant Tender, there seems to be a separate wing of rooms attached to the main house by a covered walkway. The main house is lit up like there's a party going on, but the separate wing is mostly blacked out with low lighting in one or two rooms. That'd be my guess as to where they've stashed Tory. But something else is going on there, too." Lucas straightened with determination. "That wing had mystical energy protecting it alone. I've said the chants that will break through the magic there, too."

"I want to try reaching Tory," Cisco said. "A quick strike. In and out and back to Sunnie—she's waiting on the road. You and the rest of the Brotherhood can bash in all the heads you want after we're long gone."

"Your woman and mine are on their way here."

"What? How do you know?"

Lucas hesitated for a beat, as though he were listening to some unseen voice. "Teal called me. But I knew they had made up their minds long before I heard from them.

"You love her." Lucas said that last with such certainty Cisco was taken by surprise.

"Your wife Teal? I hardly know her." Cisco knew what Lucas had meant, but he wasn't quite ready to share his feelings, so he felt it was easier making a joke.

Lucas ignored the smart remark. "Even if you stayed together, you can't keep Sunnie safe forever. She's strong-willed and too smart. Are you afraid you'll lose her if she steps out of her darkness?"

The damned man was talking in metaphors and it made Cisco itch with discomfort. Unfortunately he also knew exactly what Lucas was talking about. And that made him uncomfortable, too.

"I can't lose her. She isn't found. Not by me. Not the way you mean. I'm not what she needs. I just want her out of the shadows and back to her life and family, where she belongs."

"If you don't plan on standing beside her, leave now. It will hurt less."

Cisco drew in air, let it out. "I do love her."

"And she loves you. But that is not always enough."

Perhaps not. But Cisco had had enough of talking in circles. He wanted to find Tory, bring her to safety, then see if there would be a chance at ending the Wolf's life.

That one action would tell Sunnie everything he felt. Then he wouldn't have to say goodbye. Leaving only meant adding one more layer of scars to his hardened heart. And he was too much of a coward to face her disappointment and pain.

"I'm going to find Tory," he told Lucas. "Try to keep Sunnie out of the worst of it, will you?"

Before he started out, Lucas taught him a code for signaling by text message. Cisco was grateful for not having to learn smoke signals or how to throw his voice the way the ancient Navajo warriors had done. There was a lot to be said for modern electronics.

He used the knife in his boot to disable a modern but simple security alarm and pry open a French door to the separate wing. Finding himself standing in an empty room that seemed to be used as a library, Cisco crept to the interior door and eased it open.

Right outside was a long, poorly lit hallway. At one end was another exterior door, presumably the connection to the main house. Also down that way, a guard sat dozing in a folding chair directly outside one of the many interior doors. His presence made it a good possibility that that room was where they were keeping Tory.

Turning his head to the other end of the hallway, Cisco spotted a huge set of double doors. To their side was a panel that looked from this distance like a circuit board with levers and buttons. Security. Something important must be housed behind those doors.

Everything was quiet. Too quiet.

Then the door he'd guessed as the connection to the main house blasted open and a couple of men walked in. They came straight toward him down the hall, striding right past the guard, who had awoken with a start and sat at attention. As they quickly passed by his hiding place, Cisco could hear them talking in a mixture of Navajo and English. The lighting was low, but he saw that one man seemed to be the other's superior.

They went straight down the hall to the double doors. One said, "You have the code, Professor?"

Cisco didn't hear the answer but knew it had been said with disdain. He wondered if the one with more authority might be Professor Yellowhorse. If so, Lucas Tso would like that information. In a few seconds the two men disappeared inside the double doors.

Taking his best chance first, Cisco used his knife to make a subdued but annoying scratching noise on the wooden door to the library, where he stood. Just loud enough to get the guard's attention. One more time and then the foolish guard got up from his chair to find out where the noise was coming from. Cisco held his breath, waited until the guard got closer, then took him down with one arm around his chest and one hand on the artery in his neck.

The guard was out of action in an instant and without

a sound. Cisco dragged the body back into the library. Then he palmed his blade again and took off down the hallway with knife in hand.

It took less than sixty seconds to reach the now-unguarded door and jimmy the lock. Inside, as he'd hoped, was a blond woman, hog-tied on a queen-size bed. The lighting was dim, but Cisco saw the fear in her eyes.

He put his fingers to his lips to motion her to remain quiet, then he bent to whisper in her ear. "Sunnie Begay sent me. I won't hurt you, but you can't make noise."

At the mention of Sunnie's name, Tory nodded her head. After Cisco slit the ropes around her ankles, he heard an involuntary groan. She must've been in that position for many hours. With cramps and numbness, this woman would never make it out of here under her own power. He finished cutting her free, then told her to lay still.

Okay. It was time to make use of his new code. He pulled out his cell, was relieved to see a strong signal and sent a message to Lucas using his thumbs. Then he went to the lone window. Within a minute's inspection of the sill he found the security system. Disabling it was tricky, but he managed.

By the time he was done with the system and had the screen cut out, two figures appeared at the window. He'd expected to see Lucas, but the first face he saw was much more familiar.

Sunnie. She hoisted herself up and climbed through the window, with Lucas right behind her.

When he had her in his arms, he gave her a scowl

of disapproval. But she narrowed her lips and shook her head. Laying one hand lightly against his chest, she looked up at him with what had to be gratitude in her eyes. Then she pulled free and went directly to Tory's side and began rubbing the other woman's arms and legs, trying to get the circulation going in her friend's limbs.

Cisco took Lucas aside. "The double doors down the hall—your professor's there, but I'm not sure we'll be able to get in."

"Wait," was all Lucas said. Then he gave him a wry smile and began sending another text message.

Turning back, Cisco saw Sunnie trying to help Tory get through the window. Right outside, the waiting arms of her husband, Dr. Ben, captured her and held her close.

When Tory was safe, Sunnie halted and turned to Cisco. "Thank you," she breathed.

"Out," he told her quietly.

"But you're coming, too."

He shook his head. In the distance, a rooster crowed three times.

Sunnie lifted her head. "Let the Brotherhood handle the rest," she urged. "It's not your fight."

Wanting one more kiss, one last moment, but knowing the touch of her lips might weaken his resolve, Cisco picked up his slender love and slid her out the open window without uttering a word. He said a prayer under his breath that she would be able to make her way to safety. *Adios, mi amor. Vaya con Dios.*

All of a sudden there was the sound of an explosion coming from the main house. Then two more in quick succession. High-pitched shouts and alarm bells began to ring out.

Cisco watched over Lucas's shoulder as the double doors at the end of the hall crashed open. Three men came charging across the threshold and raced down the hall. The last of the three was the man Cisco figured was the evil professor.

Lucas held his place and gently closed the door as the men traveled past. In another moment Lucas reopened it and stole down the hall behind the three just as the first blasted out through the connecting door.

Cisco stood in the hall, watching Lucas's back and also keeping an eye on the double doors in the opposite direction, which were still standing wide-open.

He saw Lucas catch up to the last man, the professor, just as that one changed forms. Right before his eyes, what had been a human turned into a small owl. Amazed, he knew he would never question witchcraft again.

In that instant Lucas pounced on the bird before the thing could take wing. Cisco somehow lost perspective between human and fowl. There was a jumble of motion, along with two sets of deep, masculine chants. He couldn't make out either forms or words.

Cisco decided there would never be a better time to find out what was so important behind those double doors. After he made his way down the hall, he paused and looked back toward the fading commotion at the other end. He saw Lucas standing over the carcass of a dead owl as feathers dripped slowly from his fingertips.

Hunter and Kody Long rushed through the doorway and brushed past Lucas. Perfect timing. Without a word, they halted long enough to let Cisco lead the way down the hall. The three brothers stepped through the double doors and found an alcove on the left with a bank of computers. No one sat at the machines.

Straight ahead of them a darkened room spread out. On a massive bed in the center of the room lay the form of a sick, old man. As the three of them came closer, they saw the pockmarked face that had once had Cisco's own features. A jawline and forehead were all that remained to seem familiar.

Hunter leaned over and whispered, "Kody now knows."

Cisco wasn't sure what Kody would think, but both Long brothers deserved to be here for the end.

The old man moaned slightly and raised his hand. "You came to help. Give me the parchment's instructions."

Hunter spoke up from behind Cisco. "We don't have them."

"Then I'm a dead man. Get out and leave me alone."

"Don't you recognize us, Father?" Cisco asked in a clear, strong voice. Sure the old man was too weak, Cisco knew that his mind must be gone, too.

No further words came from the blurred form lying in the bed. The vision wheezed once, then stopped breathing. Once again, right before Cisco's eyes, a human body changed forms. Skin and sinew became fur and claw, until at last what lay dead in the bed was an old gray wolf.

Cisco stood shoulder to shoulder with his two brothers, looking down at the abomination for the moment. Then, without needing to say a word, together they turned and headed out to join the rest of the Brotherhood in cleaning up the mess.

Chapter 16

He'd left without a word. More than two weeks later, Sunnie still couldn't believe Cisco hadn't even bothered to say goodbye. He'd helped the Brotherhood fight off the rest of the Skinwalkers at the mansion. Then, at daybreak he'd had Hunter drive him to the airport without looking back.

He'd left his car with the missing parts at Junior's garage, the same way he'd left her with a missing heart.

Not that she would have collapsed at his feet and begged him to take her with him if he had stopped to say goodbye. She'd known the two of them weren't meant to be together. He'd made it clear that though he might love her, he would never stay with her. For some reason, he seemed sure she was meant to be in Dinetah—without him.

Sighing, she thought about how the work of rooting out evil still continued in Dinetah. But without the Navajo Wolf and the leaders of his evil band, most of the Skinwalkers had been rounded up by the Brotherhood and were undergoing deprogramming and harmony training.

Stumbling through her memories and thoughts, Sunnie finished bandaging a child's skinned knee and put away her instruments while in a kind of autopilot mode. It was nice to be back to work at Raven Wash Clinic, even if she did keep catching stomach bugs every time she turned around. But neither work nor illness could keep her mind off the man who had helped save her entire clan from the darkness and bring them into balance.

If he didn't want to be with her, there was nothing she could do. She only wished for some way to capture a moment in time and space to bring her spirit back. A moment where the two of them could have a better ending to their story.

Sunnie had to wipe the glaze of tears from her eyes. He'd thought she was strong and special—and would have a better life without him.

"But I was only special in your eyes, Bounty Hunter," she whispered to the shadows. "Without you, I'm back to being nothing but dull and gray."

Tory Wauneka caught up to her in the hall. "Hey. You don't look so hot. Are you feeling all right?" Tory was none the worse for her kidnapping and had been helping out at her husband's clinic for the last of the winter months.

"Just a stomach thing. Must've been something I ate."

"You need rest…. Why don't you go on home?"

Yeah, home *alone.* It meant nothing to her anymore.

* * *

Six weeks later, Sunnie stepped out the back door of the clinic, trying to find some air. She was tired and needed a break, but her thoughts never strayed far from Cisco. What was he doing? Where was he now?

Then there he was, standing tall in the warm spring sunshine, next to a fancy red car. Waiting for her?

"Cisco." That one word was all Sunnie could manage past the huge lump in her throat as she closed the door behind her.

"May I speak to you a minute?" he asked.

"Sure." He didn't have to ask. She was his to do with as he wished. "I've been wanting to tell you…that is, I never had the chance to say a proper goodbye."

"Would you consider putting off the goodbye?" he asked softly. "Maybe making that a welcome back instead?"

"Back? For how long?"

He looked down at his boots like a man who was unsure of himself. Not at all like the Cisco she knew.

"For as long as you'll have me," he murmured half under his breath.

"Of course. You're welcome…" His meaning hit her then like a baseball to the Adam's apple. "What are you…saying?" she stuttered past a choking sob.

"I love you, *mi vida*. With everything I am. And I think—at least I hope—you love me, too. I thought I could live without you. Thought you'd be better off in the arms of your own family. Living your own life. But it's no good. I'm no good. I don't know a thing about families, and I'm not sure I can fit into your world. But I need to try.

"I'm useless without you," he continued slowly. "The job, the houses…none of that means a thing. I can't stand not knowing if you're all right."

Tears streamed down her cheeks and she gave up on trying to hold them back. "I do love you. You know I do. But I didn't think you'd come back. I thought I would have to find you."

He took her hand and held it against his beating heart. "You were coming to me? Isn't everything okay? Why did you need me?"

She threw her arms around his neck and laughed through the tears. "Because I want you in my world, too, Cisco. To be my life, my love, my always. And if you'll stay with me, love me back, I promise you'll have all the family you will ever want or need."

Epilogue

Cisco slipped out of the waiting room where all his family had gathered. His half brothers, Hunter and Kody, and their wives, Bailey and Reagan, chatted quietly with Mrs. James, who had become like another mother to both him and Sunnie. The rest of the Brotherhood would be coming later today. Even now, Michael Ayze's wife and sister were gathering all the children so their parents could visit.

But Cisco was on a mission. Determined to have a quiet moment with his wife and a chance to be alone with their new son, he crept down the hall and eased into Sunnie's room.

She lay in the bed, sleeping with their brand-new baby, Francisco Santiago Jr., in her arms. Cisco pulled up a chair and gazed down at his life. With his heart in his throat, he reached out to touch each of them.

How his world had changed. Nine months ago he would've never guessed it could be so different.

Up until a few weeks ago he and Sunnie had been traveling across the world. First so he could watch her face light up every time he showed her some new place or pointed out a new natural wonder. And secondly so he could work on his new assignment of tracking down the hundreds of bank accounts that the Navajo Wolf had secreted far and wide.

The Navajo Tribal Council had hired his company for the task, and though his employees were competent at most things, this was one job he wanted to handle himself. Cisco had agreed to find and bring back to the People the money the Wolf had stolen. It might end up taking years, yet he was the right man for the job.

For now, they were *home*.

As he studied his new baby, Cisco had a moment of pure terror. Was he the right man for the job as this child's father? He'd never had a good example to follow. But if love counted for anything, he would certainly die trying.

Sunnie blinked awake and gazed up at him. The love shone there in her eyes, too. It gave him strength.

He took her hand and squeezed. "He's as beautiful as you are, *mi vida*. You did good."

"*We* did good, Daddy. And your son and I love you very much."

He bit back the sudden wetness in his eyes to behold everything he had ever wanted—and not realized he'd missed until Sunnie. Love. Happiness. And, most of all, *family*.

* * * * *

For a sneak preview of Marie Ferrarella's
DOCTOR IN THE HOUSE,
coming to NEXT in September,
please turn the page.

He didn't look like an unholy terror.

But maybe that reputation was exaggerated, Bailey DelMonico thought as she turned in her chair to look toward the doorway.

The man didn't seem scary at all.

Dr. Munro, or Ivan the Terrible, was tall, with an athletic build and wide shoulders. The cheekbones beneath what she estimated to be day-old stubble were prominent. His hair was light brown and just this side of unruly. Munro's hair looked as if he used his fingers for a comb and didn't care who knew it.

The eyes were brown, almost black as they were aimed at her. There was no other word for it. Aimed. As if he was debating whether or not to fire at point-blank range.

Somewhere in the back of her mind, a line from a

B movie, "Be afraid—be very afraid…" whispered along the perimeter of her brain. Warning her. Almost against her will, it caused her to brace her shoulders. Bailey had to remind herself to breathe in and out like a normal person.

The chief of staff, Dr. Bennett, had tried his level best to put her at ease and had almost succeeded. But an air of tension had entered with Munro. She wondered if Dr. Bennett was bracing himself as well, bracing for some kind of disaster or explosion.

"Ah, here he is now," Harold Bennett announced needlessly. The smile on his lips was slightly forced, and the look in his gray, kindly eyes held a warning as he looked at his chief neurosurgeon. "We were just talking about you, Dr. Munro."

"Can't imagine why," Ivan replied dryly.

Harold cleared his throat, as if that would cover the less than friendly tone of voice Ivan had just displayed. "Dr. Munro, this is the young woman I was telling you about yesterday."

Now his eyes dissected her. Bailey felt as if she was undergoing a scalpel-less autopsy right then and there. "Ah yes, the Stanford Special."

He made her sound like something that was listed at the top of a third-rate diner menu. There was enough contempt in his voice to offend an entire delegation from the UN.

Summoning the bravado that her parents always claimed had been infused in her since the moment she first drew breath, Bailey put out her hand. "Hello. I'm Dr. Bailey DelMonico."

Ivan made no effort to take the hand offered to him.

Instead, he slid his long, lanky form bonelessly into the chair beside her. He proceeded to move the chair ever so slightly so that there was even more space between them. Ivan faced the chief of staff, but the words he spoke were addressed to her.

"You're a doctor, DelMonico, when I say you're a doctor," he informed her coldly, sparing her only one frosty glance to punctuate the end of his statement.

Harold stifled a sigh. "Dr. Munro is going to take over your education. Dr. Munro—" he fixed Ivan with a steely gaze that had been known to send lesser doctors running for their antacids, but, as always, seemed to have no effect on the chief neurosurgeon "—I want you to award her every consideration. From now on, Dr. DelMonico is to be your shadow, your sponge and your assistant." He emphasized the last word as his eyes locked with Ivan's. "Do I make myself clear?"

For his part, Ivan seemed completely unfazed. He merely nodded, his eyes and expression unreadable. "Perfectly."

His hand was on the doorknob. Bailey sprang to her feet. Her chair made a scraping noise as she moved it back and then quickly joined the neurosurgeon before he could leave the office.

Closing the door behind him, Ivan leaned over and whispered into her ear, "Just so you know, I'm going to be your worst nightmare."

Bailey DelMonico has finally
gotten her life on track, and is
passionate about her recent career
change. Nothing will stand in the way
of her becoming a doctor...that is,
until she's paired with the sharp-tongued
Dr. Ivan Munro.

Watch the sparks fly in

Doctor in
the House

by *USA TODAY* Bestselling Author
Marie Ferrarella

Available September 2007

Intrigued? Read more at
TheNextNovel.com

HN88141

REQUEST YOUR
FREE BOOKS!

2 FREE NOVELS PLUS 2 FREE GIFTS!

Silhouette® Romantic

SUSPENSE

Sparked by Danger, Fueled by Passion!

YES! Please send me 2 FREE Silhouette® Romantic Suspense novels and my 2 FREE gifts. After receiving them, if I don't wish to receive any more books, I can return the shipping statement marked "cancel." If I don't cancel, I will receive 4 brand-new novels every month and be billed just $4.24 per book in the U.S., or $4.99 per book in Canada, plus 25¢ shipping and handling per book plus applicable taxes, if any*. That's a savings of at least 15% off the cover price! I understand that accepting the 2 free books and gifts places me under no obligation to buy anything. I can always return a shipment and cancel at any time. Even if I never buy another book from Silhouette, the two free books and gifts are mine to keep forever.

240 SDN EEX6 340 SDN EEYJ

Name	(PLEASE PRINT)
Address	Apt. #
City	State/Prov.	Zip/Postal Code

Signature (if under 18, a parent or guardian must sign)

Mail to the **Silhouette Reader Service**™:
IN U.S.A.: P.O. Box 1867, Buffalo, NY 14240-1867
IN CANADA: P.O. Box 609, Fort Erie, Ontario L2A 5X3

Not valid to current Silhouette Intimate Moments subscribers.

Want to try two free books from another line?
Call 1-800-873-8635 or visit www.morefreebooks.com.

* Terms and prices subject to change without notice. NY residents add applicable sales tax. Canadian residents will be charged applicable provincial taxes and GST. This offer is limited to one order per household. All orders subject to approval. Credit or debit balances in a customer's account(s) may be offset by any other outstanding balance owed by or to the customer. Please allow 4 to 6 weeks for delivery.

Your Privacy: Silhouette is committed to protecting your privacy. Our Privacy Policy is available online at www.eHarlequin.com or upon request from the Reader Service. From time to time we make our lists of customers available to reputable firms who may have a product or service of interest to you. If you would prefer we not share your name and address, please check here. ☐

SRS07

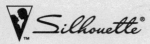

Silhouette®

Romantic
SUSPENSE

Sparked by Danger,
Fueled by Passion.

When evidence is found that Mallory Dawes
intends to sell the personal financial information
of government employees to "the Russian,"
OMEGA engages undercover agent Cutter Smith.
Tailing her all the way to France, Cutter is
fighting a growing attraction to Mallory while at
the same time having to determine her connection
to "the Russian." Is Mallory really the mouse in
this game of cat and mouse?

Look for

Stranded with a Spy

by *USA TODAY* bestselling author

Merline Lovelace

October 2007.

Also available October wherever you buy books:
BULLETPROOF MARRIAGE *(Mission: Impassioned)*
by Karen Whiddon
A HERO'S REDEMPTION *(Haven)* by Suzanne McMinn
TOUCHED BY FIRE by Elizabeth Sinclair

Silhouette® Romantic SUSPENSE

COMING NEXT MONTH

#1483 STRANDED WITH A SPY—Merline Lovelace
Code Name: Danger
When evidence suggests that Mallory Dawes intends to sell government information, OMEGA undercover agent Cutter Smith is sent to investigate. But a complex game of cat and mouse ensues as he fights his growing attraction for Mallory.

#1484 BULLETPROOF MARRIAGE—Karen Whiddon
Mission: Impassioned
Secret agent Sean McGregor fakes his own death when a madman murdered his family and targeted his wife. Now he must return from the shadows to save the woman with whom he once shared his life.

#1485 A HERO'S REDEMPTION—Suzanne McMinn
Haven
Caught in a supernatural time shift, Dane McGuire is taken back to the week of Calla Jone's death—and he'll be convicted of murder if he can't stop the past. But along the way he develops an intense desire for the woman he may ultimately kill.

#1486 TOUCHED BY FIRE—Elizabeth Sinclair
The last person firefighter Samantha Ellis wants protecting her is Detective AJ Branson. The arrogant, sexy detective spells trouble, but with a maniac out to kill her, AJ seems to be the only one who can save her—and steal her heart.

SRSCNM0907